I0677150

BAIT AND SWITCH
& other stories

ASHLEY SIEVWRIGHT

Clouds of Magellan | Melbourne

© 2020 Ashley Sievwright

First published in Australia in 2020

All rights reserved.

ISBN: 978-0-6484604-9-7 – paperback

ISBN: 978-0-6487469-1-1 – ebook

Clouds of Magellan Press, Melbourne, Australia

www.cloudsofmagellanpress.net

Production and distribution by eBook Alchemy

www.ebookalchemy.com.au

Cover and design: Gordon Thompson

Cover image: Photo by Anton Danilov | Unsplash

Author image: Hossein

CONTENTS

MY COUSIN MARK

The first thing I noticed when I moved in with my cousin Mark in Kings Cross was that he now wore a dress. It wasn't a girly dress, not frou frou or pinched at the waist, or frilled; and not worn as if he was pretending to be a girl, or trying to pass as a girl, or even in costume for some reason — but undoubtedly a dress. A shift-dress I suppose it was, straight across at the neck, hanging down from the shoulders like a cropped teeshirt, but going all the way down to mid-calf. It was black and there were beads all over it — jet-black bugle-beads, he told me later, sewn in angular patterns all over the surface.

As I was to learn in the three months I stayed with Mark, that's all he ever wore, shift dresses. When he went out he would pull on some black boots that did up over the ankles, a coat if it was cold, but never anything else at all feminine. He wore no jewellery, no makeup, had no high-heeled shoes. His hair, black and wavy and shoulder length, was often tangled. He sometimes wore it tied up in a bun, but mostly he wore it down on his shoulders, which were kind of broad, even though his arms and chest were skinny. He had hairy underarms that showed at the arm-holes of the shift, and when he went to the loo he hoiked the dress up, fished his dick out of his jocks and pissed standing up. (Not that I made a habit of watching him pee, but we did go out to clubs together now and then, and occasionally went to the urinal at the same time.) He didn't look like a girl at all, he looked just like a long-haired, skinny man in a shift dress.

There were a number of dresses he wore, but they were all much the same. I don't have a lot of knowledge about fashion, but most of them were beaded and looked to me maybe like dresses from the 20s. One shift he had, which looked more 60s to me, was sheer and satiny, a going-out shift maybe, and that one had some sort of chiffon sleeves to it. All those dresses, they were really the only feminine thing about how he chose to present himself. Although, the more I got to know him, the more I noticed a careful, swishy way he had of moving around, a kind of prissiness when arranging himself on the furniture, sort of curling his legs up sideways and half under him. He kept his knees together at all times, I noticed, just like a lady.

I don't know much about these things even now, and I certainly didn't back then, when I came to stay with him. I was so young. I didn't know anything about sexual identity, gender identity. Did Mark feel more like a girl inside than he bothered trying to look on the outside? I don't know. We never talked much, not at school, not when I came to stay with him, and certainly not about anything remotely close to gender identity. He was just Mark, always a bit of a show-pony, always a bit weird; and Mark now wore shift dresses and kept his knees together.

As far as I could tell — and again, this is only from the few months I stayed with him — he slept with both girls and boys, but probably had a preference for boys. I deduce this because when he had a girlfriend around, a friend who was a girl, I mean, they would talk about boys together, even if they did then disappear into his room at the end of the night and stay in there until morning making the usual noises. When he had a boy over it was all about him.

Mark's mum, my mum's sister, had two kids by a guy who was part-Aboriginal, so Mark had a bit of that in him — light brown skin, big dark eyes, a slightly broad nose and dark hair. 'A touch of the tar' it was called at school, and, I'm ashamed to say, at home by my own mum and dad. His dad had not stayed around, but he and his sister (they were twins) were a constant reminder of this injection of non-white into our otherwise super-white-bread family. I myself was pale as pasteurised milk and although I had brown hair, when the sun shone through the hair on my arms there was a tinge of red in there. We had English and Scottish heritage somewhere way back, but really we were just plain old pineapple-on-a-pizza Aussie.

What I find amazing, really, thinking back — trying to remember those months with any clarity, because they are a dim memory — is that Mark in a shift dress didn't faze me in the slightest. I walked in, I noticed, but I didn't notice, if you know what I mean? He was my cousin, he was in a shift dress, and I didn't give a shit. I was, at the time, 14 years old, completely self-absorbed, and my parents had just died.

*

Mum and dad died in a car accident out on a country road. All I remember about that time is how sudden and how final it all was. They were there, they were fine, then they were dead. They'd been good parents to me, I guess. I'd been a clueless kid, happy enough, if possibly a bit of a wandering dreamer all through school. They'd been coming back from the family block up in country NSW, and they got wiped out by a P-plater going too fast who wandered over into the gravel at the edge of the road, fishtailed back onto the road, clipped and flipped them. It happens all the time apparently. But like I said, they were there and all was well, and then they weren't and all was — well it wasn't like everything turned sour, it's just that it couldn't go on being the same.

At first, that's all I could think about, going on precisely the same. The day after the accident it was Monday and it was school. I got up and had a shower and got dressed in my uniform. One of mum's friend's, one of a couple who had come over to stay with me until Mark's mum, my Aunty Grace, could get down from Brisbane, she had to tell me no, I couldn't go to school. I asked why, and she did this big long explanation to me that I must admit I stopped listening to. Okay, so I couldn't go to school. Sure. I get it. But at least I was going to have my usual breakfast — Froot Loops with milk and a slice of toast with peanut butter.

When Aunty Grace got there things were a little better. She wasn't so worried about the right things to do or what people thought. She never had been. She was the first person I ever heard swear. We were out down the shops for some reason, a while back this was, when I was still a little kid, and some blokes out the front of a pub said something to her about Mark and his sister, Lulu, and she told them to 'go fuck yourselves'. I was shocked and felt instantly as if I was going to get in trouble, just for having been around and heard her say it, but secretly I loved her just that little bit more from that day forward.

Aunty Grace was also, it soon became obvious, not coping with her sister and brother in law having just died in a car accident; well, her sister at least — she'd never had much time for my dad. She cried a lot, she hugged me a lot, which I remember being super-awkward because she had quite big boobs, she reminisced a lot (about a past as a girl with my mum that sounded strangely idyllic and not like my mum at all) and she also smoked a lot of dope, which she tried to get me to share with her. I didn't, but just the fumes of the stuff got me feeling light-headed.

After the funeral Aunty Grace asked me flat out what I was going to do.

I was, I remind you, at the time just 14. I was also quite a young 14. I was, like I said, a bit of a dreamer. I didn't have heaps of friends, or do any sports or anything. I drew a lot, quite intricate artworks that took forever, and was good at writing, but other than that, I was clueless, really.

'Do?' was the best I could manage. Was it up to me? Was I out on my own?

'Yeah. What are we going to do with you?' That sounded a bit more like it might be someone else's responsibility. 'You're going to stay on at school, right?'

Did I have a choice?

'Ummm, yeah.' I wanted to. I had only just started year 10. I guess I didn't love school or anything, but I just didn't want anything to change. I wanted the same Froot Loops, the same bed, the same house, the same walk to school. I didn't want to move.

'Well, we've got to sell the house,' she said flatly, eyeing me. 'So we can fix up the estate.'

Right, I thought. The estate. They were here, my mum and dad, then they were gone, and after a few tears and a spliff we were talking about selling the house and splitting up the estate. And I was being moved.

'We'll move you in with Mark until we think of something. You can still get a train to school then. Would you like that?'

It would be a long commute from the city out to Penrith, but yeah, I would like that.

'Yeah,' I said, but she hadn't waited to hear my response. She was dialling Mark to set it up.

So that's how I came to stay with my cousin Mark in Kings Cross, even though he was only 20 years old to my 14 years. He was the only member of our extended family who lived in Sydney, apart from me and my now dead mum and dad. The rest lived in Brisbane, in Perth or overseas.

I hadn't had all that much to do with Mark while we were growing up. Back then Aunty Grace still lived close to us in Sydney, in a council flat, along with the twins, Mark and Lulu, and all three of us kids went briefly to the same schools. When I went into year 7 at Penrith High, Lulu had already left for a hairdressing apprenticeship and after that moved up to Brisbane with her boyfriend and started having babies, but Mark was still in year 12. He wasn't wearing a dress then. You couldn't at school, of course, if you were a boy — I presume, although maybe it's different now. But I do remember he pushed the envelope a bit with the uniform. His jumper was oversized and stretched and had holes in the cuffs where he put his thumbs. He wore grey school shorts all year round, and they almost disappeared under the oversized jumper. He wore black school shoes and white knee-high girls' socks that he pushed down to his ankles. He wore his hair sometimes in bunches all over his head, tied up in little bobbles with hair elastics, and earrings and amulets on leather around his neck, tied tight like chokers, which he was always being told to take off. He would lounge around on the steps to different buildings or in the breezeway. He looked like he was in a band — either that or homeless.

The girls loved him, and he could often be found lounging around with them, but the boys teased him and targeted him a lot. I was fascinated by him, but felt totally different to him, and in fact terrified of him at the same time. He was way too out-there for me. When my own school mates in year 7 twigged that I was his cousin, I got a bit of stick for it.

I got really annoyed with him for a while about that, making himself such a target, and by extension making me a target, by being so out there and effeminate. He didn't try to avoid it at all. In fact, he seemed to seek out the boys and deliberately goad them. And then they'd chase him all over the school grounds until they caught him, flatten him on the ground and kick him in the guts, punch him in the face, then dack him and try to stick something up his arsehole — a stick or something. Mark would end up bleeding and crying, snot streaming, and hobble to the Principal's office. Then he'd be off school for a bit, but not long after he returned it'd happen again.

'Why don't you just steer clear of them?' I asked him one time — not at school, but at some family do or other. Someone's birthday maybe.

'I won't be silenced,' he said, with a glint of fervour in his eye.

Of course, that didn't explain it at all. I couldn't see it at the time, but looking back on it now, I can see there's a difference between standing up for yourself and regularly seeking out the humiliation and pain of a beating.

Anyhow, one time, after a week off after a beating, he just didn't come back. I found out from mum that he'd up and left home. When next we saw Aunty Grace she told us that he had gone to live with friends in the city, in Kings Cross no less, and that he was working and seemed to be doing all right for himself.

'What's he doing?' my mum asked.

'Promotions,' Aunty Grace said, and none of us was any the wiser.

She didn't seem in the least worried about it, although I do remember after she'd gone my mum and dad being very dismissive about this 'so-called job', and scathing about Grace's parenting skills. They didn't say much in front of me, they never did, but I heard enough.

*

Mark lived in a terrace house in the backstreets off Darlinghurst Road. Back almost twenty years ago, when I went to live there, it was a complete wreck of a place. The iron lacework fence at the front that all the other terraces in that block had was gone. The front window had been broken in one section and that panel was boarded up, although the rest remained clear. Inside it was dank and dim and stank of smoke and unwashed dishes and mould. I was never quite sure how many people lived at the terrace, but there always seemed to be a lot of them around. There was a grim front room, where there was a horrible brown couch and a tele, and a kitchen which was rank because of some sort of pipe smell or something, but mostly people tended to congregate in the backyard. Out there, there was an outdoor sitting room thing going on, with old couches and poufs and umbrellas all arranged under a Jacaranda tree, with coloured lights in it. There was also a fridge that had been dragged out and powered with an extension lead to keep the drinks cold. It was, actually, really beautiful. No wonder the house itself seemed rarely occupied.

My room wasn't a room really, it was just the front upstairs balcony which had been built in, rather shoddily, with cement-sheeting, no insulation or anything, as a sort of sunroom, with louvre windows all around from about waist height up. Given it was the end of summer into early autumn when I was there, the lack of insulation didn't bother me. On hot nights, with the louvres open, I'd get the breeze coming in and right through the balcony, and it was quite fine. There was room enough for a single mattress and a bit of legroom beside it. The mattress, which was just on the tiles, no bed-base, got sweaty underneath, but it'd dry out through the day if I picked it up and leaned it against the cement-sheeting. Not that I bothered doing this very much. You got out to the balcony by climbing through one of the tall sash windows of the front upstairs bedroom, Mark's room. Mark had put shawls and sheets and blankets up, because there weren't any curtains, and they could be let down to give me complete privacy out on the balcony.

At first, I spent my time between school and the balcony, just lazing on my mattress, drawing, listening to CDs on my Walkman. I had some money and I kept myself in Froot Loops and milk, and that was all. The rest of the time Mark would get us something to eat, or really late at night we might get leftovers brought home by one of the housemates who worked at KFC. I have never had so much corn as I did during that time — for some reason there always used to be a lot of corn on the cob left at the end of her shift. Still, when my Aunt Margaret, the other of mum's sisters, the one who lived in Perth, rang me to see how I was getting on, she asked if I was eating vegetables, and I was able to tell her perfectly truthfully that yes, I was. She was always trying to get me to tell her horrible stuff about Mark, and the house, and who lived there and how I was being treated, but I never said a thing. She wanted me to move over to Perth and live with her. But who wanted to move to Perth?

We never cooked anything in that vile kitchen, that's for sure. I don't think I ever even opened the inside fridge. I kept my milk in the beer fridge out the back, pushed in behind the beers. I would bring a bowl of cereal down and have it in the garden every morning before heading out to school. And I did keep going to school. The commute out to Penrith was a bitch, but I did it. Well, to begin with, I did. Things slackened off a bit as the weeks went by, I admit.

In short, it was fine being there. I felt okay. Well, I mean, I didn't feel okay at all, but I didn't feel awful. My little rectangle of balcony and louvre windows gave me all the privacy I needed. Even climbing in the window of a morning in my school uniform with a bowl of Froot Loops in my hand, and moving through the room when Mark was asleep in there — well, passed out on his bed — I didn't even mind that so much.

Mark was ... Well, I find it hard to know what he was, actually. I didn't speak much to him. I didn't take the time. But he was easy, maybe that's the word. He never said things to me. He never seemed to notice me much, but if he did he did it in a way that didn't seem intrusive or instructive. It seemed to me at the time that adults couldn't see someone my age without telling them what to do — teachers, parents, anybody. An idle 14 year old was merely waiting to be told to do something. Mark simply left me alone. Okay, so it might not have been the textbook best thing to do with an underage boy who'd just lost his parents — Aunt Margaret certainly thought so — but in hindsight I think it was perfect. I wonder if Mark knew he was doing the right thing, or whether he got it right completely by accident, like fortuitous disinterest.

Eventually, as I said, I started going to school less. And I began partying more. There were parties at the terrace almost every weekend. Not so much full house parties, as such, but gatherings of people having pre-drinks before going out, then coming home in the early hours of the morning for chill-out sessions. At midnight, though, when they went out to the clubs, it might be utterly dead for a few hours before they came back and started up again. It was a strange clock they lived on. I began sitting with them out in the backyard as they gathered for pre-drinks. Most of the time I'd go to bed when they went out, and just ignore the chill-out stuff, but sometimes I'd join them for that as well. I did nothing but sit alongside them. I said very little.

It was a mixed crowd, and to me it didn't seem particular gay, which, given Mark's shift dresses, I might have expected. If anything, it just seemed plain rough. There was sometimes trouble out the back, arguments, once a fist-fight. I'm not sure why all these people came together, but they did. There were sometimes drag-queens, but only sometimes, and they were more dolled up, wearing wigs and makeup, not wearing a dress like Mark was wearing a dress, just a beaded shift with boots. He remained something apart, something very separate and different to the rest, and yet he fitted in with all of them.

When anyone asked who I was, Mark pounced on them, fiercely, as if they'd trashed me.

'He's my cousin. Leave him alone.'

But generally they were kind enough to me. Terribly bad influences, the lot of them, of course. It was in the Kings Cross share house that I had my first beer and my first spliff. And my first kiss actually. There was this girl there one night, really late, after the others had left for the clubs. We were out the back, under the coloured lights, moaning about life and how shit it was that my parents had died. I thought I was just being a bit of a sad-sack, but she seemed really into me and my story, so I kissed her and she let me. Then I ran my hand up her leg under her skirt and she let me. I fingered her a bit — at least I think I did, but I might have just touched her on the outside of her undies — I certainly felt something hot and dampish — but then the others came home and we broke it up. I found out later that she was in fact there with some other guy, her boyfriend, and I spent the rest of that night (well, morning) completely shitting bricks thinking he was going to bash me. But they disappeared at some point and I never saw her again. Still, a first kiss and a bit of fingering — not bad for 14.

As for Mark, he was always out, every night from Thursday through to Sunday, without fail. I remember sometimes he would play a Madonna album over and over again — the greatest hits one with all the early songs on it — and he'd be twirling around his room, 'getting ready', for hours, just off his nut. Other evenings, 'off nights', he was often out also, but this was usually at odd times, very late. He had a Nokia flip phone, which for some reason he called Ursula, and he was always getting calls on that — he never had the ring tone on, but I'd always hear it buzzing on the bedside table-top from my balcony, and a minute later hear him go out. I don't know what he did, I don't know what this 'promotions' thing was all about, but it seemed to me with his lifestyle and his phone buzzing, and his late nights out, that it was something a bit grubby. Drugs? Prostitution? To be honest, I just didn't think about it all that much.

One night, after Ursula had buzzed and Mark had disappeared, one of Mark's friends snuck me in to a club. Mark was already there, it turned out, and he didn't see me come in. I was amazed at how popular he was. He was a tear-up on the dance floor in his boots and with his hair flying around. Others flocked around him. Regular looking guys, and by regular I mean not wearing a dress, came up to him and danced at him — others, drag queens, girls, lots of people. After a while he came off the dancefloor dripping with sweat, and rank with it. He saw me and went ape-shit.

'Listen, if you wanna come out, you come out with me. These fuckers are arseholes.' He swept his arm around, indicating — well, indicating everyone. So, from then on I'd sometimes go out to the clubs, but it would always be with Mark.

He would occasionally pick up, and it seemed to be the regular looking boys that he was after, the tougher ones. It was these boys that he and his girlfriends would gripe and moan about and pine for when they weren't around, and then totally devote themselves to when they were around.

Of course, when he picked up, the balcony was out of bounds for me, and I'd just watch tele until I fell asleep on the couch in the front room. No-one seemed to mind.

One of Mark's guys, I don't remember his name, was around a lot when I was there. Well, for the last few weeks or so. It didn't seem to be a great relationship and I heard a bit of arguing in the bedroom, a bit of furniture falling over. He was a tough nut, that one, with muscles, too-high pants with a big thick leather belt, and a shitty attitude. I thought he was a dickhead, but Mark was nuts for him.

I asked Mark at one point whether this guy — I wish I could remember his name, cos it was something really odd and old-fashioned, like Arthur or something — I asked whether he, this Arthur guy, ever hurt him.

'Honey,' Mark said — he sometimes talked like a head-waggling African American woman caricature he'd seen on TV. 'There ain't no way nobody is going to lay a hand on me and live to tell the tale.' But the way he primly put his feet up on the couch, to the side, ankle to ankle — he seemed a lot more fragile than those words suggested.

Arthur disappeared a week or two later.

'It didn't work out,' Mark said, with a shrug when I asked where he'd got to.

I only saw him once more, the Arthur guy, and when I did he was looking sorry for himself and had the puce coloured remnants of a black eye. I wondered, then, whether Mark had done that, and whether all the furniture flying and blows landing were on the other side.

*

Most of the time, if Mark wasn't drunk or out of it on drugs, he was in the process of getting drunk or out of it on drugs. I saw him smoke weed, and I'm pretty sure I saw him washing pills down with beers every now and then, but I never saw him inject anything. That doesn't mean he didn't, of course.

I remember one night I woke up out on the balcony, in my little cement-sheeting room, to the sound of something going on in the kitchen. Pots and pans clanging, and the sound of some sort of pulling or splintering that seemed to come to me through the walls.

I pulled on some tracksuit pants and went to see what it was.

It was Mark, off his tits, trying to get the stove away from the wall. He was pulling it, just pulling at it. Things had fallen off the top and even though something was connected between the back of the stove and the wall, he just kept pulling.

I grabbed his arms and jerked them away.

'Stop it. What are you doing?'

'No, you don't understand. I had a tab. I'm SURE I had a tab and I think it's fallen behind the stove.'

'Why was it on the stove?'

'It wasn't.'

He started to pull again, and again I grabbed his arms.

'Where was it?'

'It was in the lounge. In that tray on the bookcase. I had it there. Dom was here but he wouldn't have taken it, and I just know I had it.'

'Did you bring it into the kitchen, though?'

He paused for a second. His eyes, big and black, glassy, wobbled, and it looked like he was going to burst into tears. But then, after a second, he looked crafty and suspicious.

'I could have,' he said darkly, as if it was a conspiracy. He nodded. 'I could have.'

I went for a quick recce in the front room and outside, but there was no tab that I could find. Not that I knew what one would have looked like, I admit. Meanwhile, he started pulling at the oven again. I couldn't stop him, so instead I helped him do it safely. There was no tab behind the stove. Unfortunately, what there was behind the stove was a slight gap between the skirting board and the wall.

'It could have fallen down there,' he said.

'No,' I said. 'It didn't fall down there. Come away. Go to bed.'

'It's down there.'

'It's not.'

'It is.'

This went on for a bit. Then, stupidly as it turns out, I said: 'If it's down there the cockroaches have it now.' We had seen a few cockroaches in the kitchen, just one or two, nothing horrific for Kings Cross, but still, we knew they were in there somewhere. Mark, unfortunately, took this as gospel. He looked crafty and suspicious again.

'Those fucking cockroaches,' he said.

I thought it best to minimise the damage, and, given we didn't have a hammer, we got a few kitchen utensils, a knife and a dirty egg-flip, and jimmied off the skirting board which was half falling off anyhow. Surprise surprise, no tab.

Of course, that didn't help, because then Mark just presumed that it had slid further down, perhaps into the wall cavity, or under the flooring. He looked, for a moment or two, utterly capable of dismantling the entire kitchen. But then, out of the blue, he had another idea about a stash of drugs that he was sure was somewhere else, and left the kitchen for his bedroom.

I put the kitchen back together — well, roughly. I just propped the skirting board back up and pushed the oven back in against it. Not a single other person had descended from the bedrooms upstairs. Not one.

When I went to check on Mark he was sprawled on his bed out cold. His shift, the one with the jet-black bugle-beads, lay at the foot of the bed. He'd stepped out of it and fallen face down. He had shit himself. Not badly. Just a little squirt it seemed, a rather hefty skid-mark up and down his undies. Non-existent tabs of acid, I could manage, but he could deal with his own skid-marks. I left him and went back to bed.

When I woke the next morning, he was in the shower and, later, when he came out, his hair wrapped in a towel, he seemed to have no memory of the night before — either that or an enviable ability to pretend nothing had happened.

*

You might be wondering about me. You might be wondering how I was getting on, grieving for my parents and stuff. And I find it really hard to tell you how I was getting on with that to be honest.

I missed my parents, of course. Sometimes I missed them like mad. I missed home, I missed all the things I knew, the routines and the unthinking blandness of life. The ease of it. But I hadn't cried — I don't think I'd cried. Not at all. Not even at their funeral when everyone was bawling their eyes out. It had been too sudden. They had gone but I wasn't different. I was precisely the same. It felt — it just didn't feel sad.

I did notice, though, even at the time, that my drawings were getting a bit — I don't know how to describe it, maybe a bit dark and nasty somehow. I also notice, looking back, how ready I was to drop days at school, after wanting so desperately not to leave; how much I was ready to drink when Mark and his friends got me in, underage, to clubs; and how little I cared about whether I was out of it or straight, going to school or not, getting up or not getting up. I didn't care. I only realise now, looking back, trying to remember that time, that I must have been numb. I didn't want anything to change, and yet I didn't want to do any of those old things anymore. I was in an odd place.

*

The last night I spent at Mark's place started off pretty routine. A few of us were out the back when Ursula buzzed on the table top and Mark said he had to go out. At the time there was a sleazy guy propped on a couch, a friend of another tenant, who had earlier in the night given me a real hard time. He'd said he wanted to pop my cherry and grabbed my dick and balls through my jeans and squeezed, which had hurt like mad. It wasn't a caress like he was trying to seduce me, it was an attack, and it hurt. Mark hadn't liked that much, and he shouldered the sleaze out of the way and told him to leave me the fuck alone. He took me aside and told me that while he didn't feel he could kick the guy out given he was a friend of the house, I should just steer clear of the dirty bastard. So, after Ursula buzzed and Mark said he had to go out, he paused for a minute, then said to me:

'Get up. You're coming.'

I did as I was told and slouched out after him. We walked down the road to a McDonalds where we got some cheeseburgers and a large Coke with ice each, then to a multi-level carpark nearby where Mark unlocked a sleek silver car — not anything too fancy, but still, a lot more sleek than I imagined Mark having. I jumped in the passenger side, kept my mouth shut, and munched on the burger. We drove to a flat a suburb or two away, then Mark made a quick call on Ursula, said, 'We're here', then told me to jump in the back. A minute or two later a man came out and got in the front. He looked like he went to the gym a lot — massive arms in a tight little tank-top. He smelled like he was fresh out of the shower, and his hair was combed flat against his head. I could see the comb marks in it. He turned around and gave me the once-over.

'Who's he?'

'My cousin. Leave him alone.'

'He's a bit young, isn't he?'

'He's just along for the ride.'

'Righto. Whatever.'

We drove this guy to a big house in another suburb.

18

'An hour, right?' Mark asked as the guy opened the door and swung a leg out.

'Yeah,' the guy said. 'I'll buzz you if he wants to go longer.'

He then walked up the drive and knocked on the door. A little light went on inside, and then the door opened and our guy was ushered inside by another man. This second man clocked us sitting in the car and shut the door quick smart. I got out of the back seat and returned to the front passenger side.

'So,' I asked. 'We wait?'

'Yeah. Sorry,' Mark said.

'Can we have the radio?'

Mark opened the glovebox and got a little transistor radio out.

'I've run the car battery down before,' he said.

So instead we turned on the transistor radio and kept it on low.

Sure, I was only 14 and I was a bit naïve with it, but even I knew what was going on right in front of my eyes. To ask questions about it would make me seem like a fool, so I just acted like we all knew exactly what was what. When Mark cracked the window and lit a smoke, I asked if I could have one, too. He said, sure, and popped one out of the soft pack for me. I wasn't very good at smoking, and I didn't really like it, but you have to do something while you're sitting in a car waiting for a male prostitute to service a client.

The closest streetlight was a little way away and no-one seemed to have their porch lights on in this street — it was virtually pitch black. We were just two shadows sitting side by side in a parked car staring out the windscreen.

'So, you're a pimp, then?' I asked him.

He snorted a laugh out of his nose.

'Just a driver tonight,' he said, and I noticed the qualification.

'What am I, then?'

'You're security,' he said.

We both smirked a bit, and I felt like I was the coolest kid in the world right then. I remember that. I remember smiling to myself, tilting my head back and squinting at the sting of the cigarette smoke, chin up, peering out the windscreen at the world and thinking, yeah, I was in it, I was living. For the first time in a long time I felt good. I shook the ice around in my Coke and took a sip. I felt amazing.

We did nothing but listen to music and smoke and make desultory conversation for the better part of the hour. We talked about the music we were listening to, the singers, and whether or not we fancied them, then we talked about actors we fancied, and people we'd turn gay for — but that game wasn't really going to work, Mark said, because he was bisexual and I was a virgin, so it was all just academic anyhow. We spent the hour just chewing the fat. It was good.

When the hour was almost up, I got out for a sneaky piss in the John's front garden, and when I got back in the car, Mark asked me something completely out of the blue.

'Are you okay?' he asked.

'What do you mean? With what?'

'Everything. Your mum and dad.'

'Yeah,' I said.

'Are you sure?'

'Yeah, I'm sure.'

Mark nodded for a bit, and took a drag on his cigarette.

'I'm not sure that's a good thing,' he said after a while. And the way he said it, not critical or anything, just making an observation, it allowed me to answer in kind.

'Nah,' I said. 'Probably not.'

Why was he doing this? Ambushing me like this when I was feeling so on top of the world? It was as if he knew how I was feeling and timed his side-swiping attack for the moment when it would catch me most unawares.

'Margaret called again today,' he said.

'I'm not going to Perth,' I said, matter of fact.

'She's been to the courts to get an order.'

I felt a burning anger well up in me then, a massive feeling of frustration and unfairness. There was no way, no way on earth I was going to Perth.

'I won't go,' I said.

Mark nodded, but said nothing.

'Fuck Perth. Fuck you all. You can't make me do it.'

'Hey,' Mark threw his hands up in front of his face. 'Don't go spitting Coke at me, honey. I'm not makin' you do nuthin'.'

I sat back in my seat.

'What order?' I asked.

'I dunno. Guardianship or something. You're only a minor.'

'I'm not going,' I said yet again. I fumbled around at the door, trying to find the handle. It was so dark on that street, and there was a blur of tears in my eyes. I felt so hijacked.

'Stop that,' Mark said and he reached over and took my wrist. I shook him off but didn't try and get out of the car.

'Listen,' Mark said. 'She's coming with that order tomorrow, okay? Probably with cops. I didn't have to tell you but I have. If you're there when they come, you're going with them, no question. I'm sorry, but you are. If you don't wanna go, you're gunna have to disappear, make your own way somehow. But can I tell you something? Can I tell you something really important? You don't wanna have to make your own way around here at your age. You really don't.'

'I do.'

'No,' he said grimly. 'Trust me.'

I sat back, sullen and sulky, the injustice of it all washing around in me and making me want to punch someone — not Mark, but maybe the guy inside, the John, or that fuckwit back at the house who'd grabbed and squeezed my nut-sack. Yeah, him.

'Oh fuck,' Mark said, interrupting my thoughts of physical violence.

'What?'

'It's been over an hour.' He grabbed Ursula from the console and double-checked the time, checked for messages, but of course there were none — we would've heard the vibration. 'Shit,' he said.

'What's the matter?'

He pressed a few buttons and put the phone to his ear. I could hear the dial-tone on the other end. He let it ring for a bit then snapped Ursula closed.

'What's the matter?' I asked again.

'We've had trouble with this John before. We have to go in.'

'We have to what?'

'I wasn't joking about being security. We have to go in. Either you call or you come out, that's the rule. Something must have happened.' He flapped his hand at me. 'So, go on,' he said.

'What, me?' My voice rose to pre-pubescent levels.

'I can't do it — I'm wearing a dress.'

'I can't do it — I'm only a minor.'

At that moment, the door of the house cracked open and the gym-built guy slipped out and down the drive to the car. By the time he got there, Mark and I were pissing our pants laughing.

'What?' the gym-built guy asked when he got there. 'What's the joke?'

Mark made him get in the back, and then we took off, hooting and hollering and laughing like it wasn't 2am in the morning in Vaucluse.

*

The three of us went out after the job was done, me and Mark and the prostitute guy who turned out to be called Gavin, of all things. We went to the one club where they seemed a bit slack about checking for ID, and where I'd snuck in before, and we danced the rest of the night away. Mark was slaying it on the dancefloor as usual, all hair-flippy and arms-in-the-air, and Gav did more than alright pulling other men who looked a lot like him. I had a go on the floor myself, even though I never usually danced. At first I felt super-awkward and uncoordinated, but then I just went for it, in all my super-awkward uncoordinated glory, until I was slick with sweat and smashing it like it was a boxing ring.

When we got home it was about 6am and I went straight out onto my little balcony, fell back on my single mattress and looked up through the louvres at the sky. I didn't feel in the least like I could go to sleep.

A few minutes later, Mark came through the window, stumbling a little, getting his feet caught up in the curtains he'd rigged up. He wasn't written off, but he'd had quite a few gin and tonics. He'd never done this before, come out of his bedroom into my little domain. I didn't mind, though. He sat on the end of the mattress and grabbed my feet. He was swaying a bit from side to side, and sort of used my feet to steady himself. The balcony seemed completely miniscule with two people in it.

'Great night,' he said, a little bit slurry.

'Yeah,' I agreed. 'Great night.'

'Yeah,' he said. 'We're all right up here, aren't we? We're okay — in this little fuckin' cubby hut thing. We're good.' He nodded a bit, wobbled, grabbed at my feet.

'I'm gunna go,' I said. 'I've decided.'

'Yeah,' Mark nodded. 'Good choice. There's nothing for you here.'

I didn't say anything to that. I didn't agree, but I didn't say anything. Aunty Margaret and the cops came to get me later that day. I went without a peep. Mark was still passed out on his bed. When I think back to that day, I wish I'd at least woken him up and said goodbye, said thank you, or left a note or something, or rang later when I got to Perth. But I didn't say anything, I didn't write anything, I didn't ring.

It seems unforgivable, and I have twinges of regret and guilt about it now, but in the years after moving out of Mark's place and going to Perth, I barely thought about him. My couple of months living with him were a blip between a perfectly ordinary, regular, happy childhood in Penrith and perfectly ordinary, mostly happy teenage years and adulthood in Perth. It's not that I blocked those in-between days out, it's just that they were so very different to the rest of my life that they didn't seem like my own memories. They seemed like a movie I'd seen a while back, or something that had happened to someone else.

I guess it makes sense. I was so lost those few months. I was numb. I closed down the day I heard mum and dad were dead, and I didn't open up again until that night, I think, the night on the dancefloor, punching the lights.

STAY AND DEFEND

One night seven winters ago, in front of an open fire, with a ragout in their bellies and wine in their glasses, Paul and Ricky had agreed that they would from then on stay during the fire season and defend their property rather than evacuate.

The first couple of years after they had bought the property in the Kinglake Ranges, up in the eucalypt forests just over an hour out of Melbourne, they had not stayed when fire threatened, but evacuated during days of high fire danger, or when fires were already burning, even if not close. At that point they did not have any animals to worry about, they had not put any major funds into renovating, and they had comprehensive home and contents insurance that included fire, so why stick around? Plus, they had a place in Melbourne to decamp to.

Ricky had kept the flat he had been paying off when he and Paul first met, way back in 1999. They had picked each other up in Three Faces, the biggest Melbourne gay club at the time, now defunct, and gone back to Ricky's flat for a drunken and totally unsuccessful shag. The next day, nursing massive hangovers, they were about to part company and write each other off — but instead they'd given it another go, just in case, and had, unexpectedly, amazing sex. This sustained them for the first six weeks, while they got to know each other, and they'd been together ever since. For many years after meeting they enjoyed hangover sex the most. It held the memory of their first sweet discovery of each other.

When they first moved up to the property, Ricky had driven there every night after work, an hour and 15 minutes on the road, and only stayed in the flat if he had a work function in the evening, or tickets to see a show. But things had shifted over the years, and by the summer of the big fires, he was staying in town pretty much all the working week and only coming home on a Friday night, sometimes on a Saturday morning. Paul worked from home, and so he was able to stay at the property all the time, and he only travelled to Melbourne when he and Ricky had plans.

Ricky's friends often stayed over in the Melbourne flat, either with him during the week, or by themselves on the weekends it was vacant. These friends of Ricky's, some his clubbing buddies from the old days, were the same age as Ricky, but they seemed to Paul so much younger. Paul, almost a decade older than Ricky, felt a generation older than these friends. It was as if they did not deign to bother with adult things like jobs and home ownership — although they must, presumably, have had both. Their youthful disdain was at odds with their lazy, sleek sophistication. One girl, Liza (with a z, although pronounced 'Lisa'), a beautiful woman, with naturally kinky blonde hair that always looked slept-on and smelled dirty-but-perfumed, looked at Paul out of eyes squinted against her cigarette smoke as if she thought absolutely nothing of him. The others he could cope with, but Liza unsettled him. It occurred to Paul, when he thought about it, that it wasn't Ricky's friends themselves, with their louche ways, even Liza with her cigarette-smoke sneer, that unsettled him, it was the fact that Ricky seemed to think so much of them.

'I know you don't like them,' Ricky had eventually said.

It had been a Saturday afternoon, and they were all packed and ready to put their bags into their good car, the BMW. They were due at Liza's birthday celebration dinner in the city, and a night in the Melbourne flat afterwards. Paul wasn't aware of being sulky about it, but he must have been. Ricky wasn't upset; he had said it lightly, sweetly, and with a little bit of amusement in his voice.

'You don't have to come. I don't mind. I really don't.'

Paul had felt shamefaced but incredibly grateful. He took his bag out of the car without a word and found himself standing on the veranda waving Ricky off, with the prospect of pottering and binge-watching TV shows stretching out in front of him for the rest of the weekend. It had been a long time since they'd spent a weekend apart, but from then on it happened a lot more often.

*

By the summer of the fires, it had got to the point where, when they were together, there were untucked edges, as if things were starting to misalign. When Ricky was up at the property, he would be surprised by some of the work Paul had done — a new deck, the chicken coop moved to a different spot. Sometimes he would stand and stare out at the trees, the trees they had both loved, with a strangely blank look on his face as if he was wondering what he was doing there. When Paul was in the city with Ricky he felt less and less at ease with eating out or with wine bars, and found Ricky talking about things he had done with or said to people Paul didn't even know.

'Who's Marty?'

'Oh, just someone from work.'

27

They were, rather generally, planning to go on a grand holiday together to celebrate their next anniversary although no tickets had been booked. They had not had a chance to really sit down together and decide where to go, although Paul had mentioned a cruise to Alaska, and Ricky was talking about staying with friends in the South of France, or skiing with the same friends in Italy. When Paul thought about the anniversary holiday, he thought about it as if it were something rumoured but unsubstantiated. It was the Loch Ness Monster of anniversary trips.

And so it came as no surprise to Paul, none at all, that when the time came to stay and protect the property from the threat of bushfire, Ricky wasn't actually there to do it with him.

*

Paul had been regularly checking the CFA website. The satellite pictures showed the fire front alarmingly close, but the roads were clear to evacuate. A notification on the site told residents there was still time, but that if the fire front changed direction — there was a change in wind direction due late that afternoon — then the roads may become impassable. They should make up their mind to stay or go now.

Paul had decided to go. Without Ricky there, he wasn't sure he wanted to stay and protect the property. Not by himself. If Ricky had been there, he would have felt more determined to go through with it, it would have felt worthwhile, but without him it seemed pointless to put himself in danger. If they weren't saving it together, there was no reason to save it. He didn't quite put it to himself in those terms, but he felt it.

Outside it was ominously silent. There was a very hot wind from the north, heated as it travelled across the vast red centre of the country, but it was not as blustery as it had been in previous days. Still, after days of this, a whole month of this, everything was tinder-dry. It didn't need much to send the fire in a new direction.

The sky was a murky grey-brown, and there was smoke in the air around him, hanging like mist around clumps of trees and squatting in the distance. He couldn't see as far as the end of their long drive for the smoke. It was thick in his nose and stuck in his throat like phlegm.

He had hosed the house down, blocked the gutters and filled them with water, had long ago removed all leaf matter and dead branches from around the house. He had left the generator on, sucking water from the pool to the sprinklers around the house, and two on the roof. It was time for him to go.

He tried to ring Ricky to let him know that he was leaving, that he was on his way down to the city, but he couldn't get a signal.

Paul slipped in to the driver's seat of the 4WD. He had the chickens in cages on the tray at the back. They were tame and had been easy to catch. The dogs were on the back seat, two labs. The young one, stupider, was snoozing, but the older one sat stately and alert, either to the danger of the fire or to Paul's own mood of quietly coiled tension. The other animals had been moved a week ago, when the fires had started, to a friend's farm in a location thought to be out of danger.

He turned the key in the ignition and the 4x4 roared into life. 'Believe' by Cher began to blare out of the speakers. Paul's iPhone was connected via Bluetooth and, for some reason, every time the car started the iPhone automatically reverted to that single song. It drove him crazy and he didn't know how to stop it. He didn't even like the song, but Ricky loved Cher and had loaded the album onto all their devices. 'Believe' was, so Ricky told him, playing in the club the night they met.

Paul jabbed at buttons on the console and turned the music off altogether. There was only the sound of the engine idling and the chickens.

He pulled away from the house and took the drive at a smooth and regular pace. In the rear-view mirror, he took a last look at the house, but it left him unmoved. Either the house would survive and he would be back here and all would be the same, the same dishes would be in the sink for him to wash, and their life would go on, his and Ricky's life, or it would burn down and he would never return. It would be one or the other. It didn't matter to him. As long as the chickens and the dogs were okay.

*

The house itself was a split-level structure built on a hillside in dense bushland. The upper level was a garage, bathroom, laundry, spare bedroom and a large kitchen, which looked over into a massive lounge and deck area. Other bedrooms were on that second level. Down another level were various sheds and basements, one of which was a spidery wood shed, stocked for winter fires in the open fireplace. With its slanted ceilings and exposed wood and brick, it was a very 70s house when they first bought it, but they installed new glass sliding doors to the deck, plastered some of the walls, completely re-did the kitchen and bathrooms, and turned it into something more modern.

It had been a shared project, and for the years they were doing it, slowly, bit by bit, driving up each weekend with tiles to lay or plants

for the garden, they both got an enormous amount of satisfaction out
of it. Those were happy days, and their routine was working perfectly,
they felt. They lived together in the Melbourne flat in those days, and
weekended in the bush. They were rarely apart.

Regularly, on weekends at the house, they would drink wine with
dinner and then more wine afterwards, watching films on the TV,
rolling off to bed thoroughly drunk with nothing more than a peck on
the cheek, but knowing that the entire morning the next day was free,
so they could laze around and re-live the hangover fuck that was their
first.

Although they had cleared the land immediately around the house
and re-planted it with banks of shrubs, a kitchen garden, a rock garden
with wildflowers in spring — beyond the garden was bush, densely
packed with eucalypts. They grew close and tall, often with trunks
rising up as high as three or four storeys, with no branches until the
upper canopy where they finally splayed out and meshed with each
other to entirely shade the land below.

It was dim in winter, and quite damp, but in summer it was cool
and shaded, apart from those days when the wind blew hot and
exhausted from the north.

In the summer the bark came loose on the eucalypts. It hung in
long thin strips up and down the trunks, but still, for a time, connected
at the top and bottom, before eventually it fell to the ground. In that
between time, those strange flaps of bark would move in the wind,
ripple, get a wriggle going, and they would flap rhythmically against the
virgin wood of the trunk underneath the old bark. There would be a
slow slapping sound as they started up: *slap slap slap*, and then when the
wind picked up it would increase to a frenzied: *slapslapslapslap*.

When he first heard this Ricky looked at the trees, cocked his head and smiled.

'The trees are wanking,' he said.

When the renovations were finished they started inviting groups of friends up for dinner parties, and there followed quite a few years of very content and satisfied nesting. They invited up mostly Paul's friends; other home-owners, married couples, gay or straight. Ricky was a great host, genial and thoughtful, a good cook. Paul got a great deal of pleasure seeing him as host, casually touching everyone as he spoke to them, putting his arm along their shoulder perhaps, just as he had always done.

Ricky hadn't changed at all. Well, not much. His face, which had once seemed pretty and almost disconcertingly feminine, had somehow set nicely as he got older, into a patrician stylishness that made him arguably more attractive than he had been in his youth. He had kept his hair and kept fit. Paul had filled out a lot more; he was now carrying a bit of a belly, but he was still strong and solid and carried the air of calm dependability he always had.

Ricky occasionally invited his own friends up, those old clubbing buddies, including Liza, but not very often as they weren't really into weekends in the country. The last time this group came up they arrived ridiculously late, too late for dinner, already drunk — they had got lost, apparently — and only stayed for a single long night of drinking and, Paul suspected, drug-taking, before they returned to town. Liza had eyed him as usual throughout the night, and the next day, when they were making their unexpectedly early departure, she had taken him aside, smelling of stale smoke and perfume, smiling, and had said:

'What is it you want with our Ricky? Hmmmm?'

And with that ridiculous parting comment, she had climbed into the back of their car, put her sunglasses on and stared straight ahead. But Paul had got used to this over the years. There was something about Ricky that made people presume he was going to be taken advantage of, something that made people want to protect him, or defend him.

Ricky did not accompany his friends back to town on that occasion, although he did give them the key to the Melbourne flat. When they had gone he refused to speak ill of them. In fact, he did not speak of them at all. He busied himself with bits and pieces of work to be done around the property the day they left, and Paul very sensibly judged it wise not to mention the great Liza abandonment, although he was pleased, quietly, to see them fall from grace, if only for a moment.

*

The road from their house was, to begin with, a twisting road cut into the side of the ridges. There were more of those tall straight-up-and-down trees with the canopy high above, and beside the road there were man ferns, with their massive brown furred trunk and umbrella of leaves. There were driveways at regular intervals and occasionally the glimpse of a house.

Paul drove at a regular speed, perhaps the slightest bit slower than he might otherwise do, and looked up every single driveway to see how many people remained. Apart from the occasional vehicle parked in a driveway or in front of a roller door he saw no sign of habitation at all. All houses were closed up, some with shuttered windows. He wondered how many people had stayed, how many had gone. How many of those houses he passed with the shuttered windows contained people, families, a husband and a wife, maybe, an elderly couple. There were a large number of retirees up in the hills.

What was obvious was that no-one was on the roads. No-one had left it this late to evacuate it seemed. Still, there was no escalation of warning on the radio, and the haze of smoke, although it coloured the sky, causing a premature duskiness, and hung in the canopy, and forever beyond the next turn, was no worse than it had been back at the house.

After the first fifteen minutes of twisting roads, there was a break in the hills, and the road straightened out across a mostly flat high plain of farmland between two long wooded ridges, just for five minutes or so, before entering the hills again and descending further to the township where there was relative safety. It was a beautiful place usually, a breath of fresh air after the close twists of the mountain, opening out and offering a view of the two distant ridges.

It was as he was driving across the high plain that he saw the kangaroo. It was travelling at half-speed along the side of the road to his right, and picked up pace when it saw the car, veering across the road from right to left in front of the car without warning. Paul had seen it in plenty of time and was going slow enough to be able to brake. The kangaroo hopped over the fence to the left and off across the farmland.

Paul looked up at the ridge to the right and saw an ominous grey-brown cloud of smoke, billowing in super-slow motion like cumulous clouds. It was the first he had seen of the smoke other than the general haze in the air, which was accumulated smoke from the previous days of fire — but this, the billows he saw above the ridge, that was smoke directly from the fire front. It was impossible to tell how far away the fire was, but while it gave him a jolt of panic, it seemed far enough away not to be immediately dangerous. After all, hadn't he seen this on the satellite picture before he left? Hadn't he known he would drive alongside the front like this in order to get out of the hills? It was, the more that he thought about it, a comfort to see the front more or less where he had expected to see it. It made this drive of his seem well-considered and easily manageable. The fire was no longer an abstract concept, it was a concrete reality and it was off over the ridge. He was going to make it down just fine.

He was just about to accelerate when he saw more kangaroos on his right, heading for the road. He put on his brakes and came almost to a crawl, allowing them to bound across in front of the car, to the other side, away from the fire. It was a regular kangaroo crossing, here, dangerous at dusk and dawn, when they were on the move. There were yellow diamond-shaped signs with the silhouette of a kangaroo all along here, warning of the danger to motorists.

If he had been driving at the posted speed he may not have seen it, but as he was only crawling along the road, he did see it — a roo caught in the wires of the fence. It seemed almost bound length-wise, horizontal to the ground, with its legs somehow pinned together and its body suspended in the fence. There was the horrible suggestion that it was on some sort of spit, ready to be roasted.

Paul felt a jolt in his stomach. The fire, the smoke over the ridge, the safety ahead of him, and the roo — it was as if his mind triangulated the distances and the times between all of those elements in seconds. But there was no doubt really. There was no choice. He could no sooner have left the roo there entangled in the fence than he could have left the dogs or the chooks back at the house.

There was no immediate urgency, but he had to act quickly. He put the brakes on and came to a complete stop. He would see if it was alive, and if it was he would free it. If it was injured he would try and subdue it and take it with him.

He pulled over to the side of the road, put the 4x4 in park, put the hazard lights on and switched off the ignition. He reached a small toolbox from the back seat and got wire-cutters from it. Not all that strong, but they'd have to do. He also grabbed a flannelette shirt that was on the floor of the cab, a bottle of water, and was out of the car in seconds, slamming the door quickly before the dogs could get out. Instead they crowded up at the windows on that side of the car, intent and indignant.

The heat hit him in the face. There was still the heavy hot wind, but he could tell it hadn't turned yet. It was still coming from the same direction as it had been up at the house. So, no danger there — yet.

It was eerily quiet on that high plain. No birdsong, he realised. Just the sound of the gently rustling trees, benign, but ominous.

Paul walked towards the roo in the fence. It seemed smaller than the other roos that had bounded across the road, and of a slightly darker colour, younger perhaps, than the others. It had not moved at all, and did not move now. It had obviously been stuck in the fence for some time, so it was presumably not from the pack that had just crossed the road.

As he got closer he could see more clearly that the roo had somehow wound itself length-wise in the wires, which, being very loose, had virtually bound it, cocooned it. This fence, the farmland on the right, belonged to the McMahon's, an elderly farming couple who did not bother overly with upkeep. Their house was a dump, surrounded by rusted old cars and farm machinery, an ancient stump-jump plough alongside the body of a silver Nissan Pulsar with red and blue racing stripes but no windows and no wheels. It was because the wire on the fences was so slack that the roo had been able to tangle itself so completely.

When he was a step or two away from the roo it still didn't move. He took in the tangle of wire around the legs, right at the joints. The wire had rubbed, broken the skin and was now embedded in the flesh. The legs were bloody. Up close the kangaroo was not as small as it had appeared from the road. In fact, the haunches were powerful, and the chest was freakishly well-muscled. Even those comic front legs, mere sticks with black-clawed paws, seemed dangerous up close.

Paul side-stepped so he could see its head clearer. It was drawn back, pulled back by the wire, the throat taut. The mouth was flecked with foam, and the eyes — they were wide open and fringed with thick sandy-coloured eyelashes. They looked, it seemed, not at Paul, but a little to the left, as if wanting to see him, but wanting also not to look him direct in the eye. It blinked.

Paul felt another lurch in his stomach when he realised it was alive. He felt compelled to speak to it, and murmured a quiet, deep, soothing: 'It'll be all right, big fella.'

But at the sound of his voice the kangaroo in the fence tensed its muscles and thrashed around in the wire.

'Shhhh,' Paul said. 'Shhhhh.'

There was no time to be lost, no purpose in prolonging this, provoking the roo to more thrashing movements that would only further injure it. He dropped the wire-cutters within arm's length, and in a smooth movement stepped forward, threw the shirt over the roo's head with the idea this might subdue it, then knelt down beside it and clamped the upper body and neck under his arm. The roo's head was now behind his shoulder, and it made grunting frothing sounds in his ear as it continued thrashing. With his free hand Paul clamped the roo's legs to the wire at the injury, to stop the friction at the point of contact as best he could.

After a moment, held like this, close and tight against the confining wire, the roo stopped thrashing. Paul was able to examine the wire, where it cut into the roo and where it didn't. It was, he quickly decided, unlikely that he would be able to disentangle it — that would involve rotating the whole roo as if it was on a spit. No, he had to cut the strands of wire away from the wound. Then, hopefully, the roo would come free, even if there were small spears of wire still embedded in its flesh.

He took his arm away from the legs and reached for the wire-cutters. At the slight alleviation of pressure, the roo again made more fruitless bounding movements. Paul was surprised at its strength, but kept his grip. Again, after a moment, the roo stopped thrashing.

Paul reached again for the cutters. This time he retrieved them and immediately set about clipping the wire from around the bound legs. He moved quickly, without hesitation, snipped once, twice, three, and then four times. At the last snip there was a shift in the weight of the roo under his arm and he realised that he had, in fact, released it. Considering how well trussed up the roo had been, he had freed it remarkably quickly.

He had only the shortest moment of satisfaction, of relief — that hadn't taken long at all — before the roo, presumably sensing a new freedom of movement, began thrashing again, and much more vigorously than before. Paul, surprised at how much stronger it was now that its limbs were unencumbered, lost his balance and fell onto his back, dragging the roo out of the wire on top of him.

The weight of the roo was a shock; it was heavier than he had expected. It was wriggling, thrashing, bounding against him. He felt the muscles contracting and moving, rock hard, and felt the limbs strike against him awkwardly, the claws dig in painfully. The sheer force of its blows appalled him. He felt abused, degraded even, by the horrible thrashing abandon of the roo. He threw his arms wide and turned his face away, screwing up his eyes. Almost immediately the weight, the coiled muscle, the wriggle, the offence of the roo was gone.

He lay panting for a moment, letting the humiliation drain away.

When he finally sat up there was a flowing warmth over one side of his face, and the red of blood in his eyes. He put his right hand up to the side of his head and felt the wet of blood, and a strange long bubble of flesh that hadn't been there before. It took him a moment to realise that it was a fresh gash above his ear, with a horrible soft globular feel. His ear seemed also to be sitting at an odd angle, further away from his head than it usually was.

'Fuck,' he said.

He blinked away the blood, wiped his eyes with the thumb and forefinger of his left hand. But it kept coming. Quite thick. He noticed that the front of his shirt, the lap of his trousers was bright red with it.

His head began to throb, and he was aware of a gathering darkness at the back of his eyes somewhere, way back behind him, like that grey-brown smoke, lingering back there somewhere waiting to move forward. He must have taken quite a blow. He must be losing a lot of blood.

'It'll be all right,' he said aloud, just as he had said to the roo.

It had always been his role to soothe. When Ricky had been in hospital for a worrying procedure, he had said the same thing, in the same voice. 'It'll be all right' he had told him. When Ricky had lost money on an investment he had said it. When Ricky's mother had died he had said it. He was always saying it. He said it to him now, even though he wasn't there. Sitting on his arse in the middle of nowhere, bleeding from a massive flesh-wound, with his ear hanging off, he said it. Well aware that he wouldn't be in this no-man's-land halfway between staying and defending his property and evacuating in a timely manner if it weren't for the fact that Ricky was never around, was never fucking there when you needed him, ever — even in those circumstances he was still saying it to him.

The flannelette shirt was just to the side of him. He grabbed it. The bottle of water could not be too far away either. He had brought it with him from the car with the confused idea of giving the roo a drink, an idea that made him feel like a foolish city-slicker now that he had witnessed its wild thrashing. He looked around for it and found it. He poured some in his eyes and wiped his face with the shirt. Then he balled the shirt up and applied it to the wound, holding his ear against his head.

After a moment, he stood up. The gathering gloom behind him came forward, but he stood still for a beat or two and it receded again. He felt okay. He felt fine.

For the first time since he had freed the roo Paul took in his immediate surroundings. They had changed. The wind was the first thing he noticed. It was now full in his face, hot and rank with the smell of smoke. The change had arrived and it was blowing directly from the fire over the ridge towards where he now stood.

He looked up at the ridge but couldn't see it any longer. The smoke he had seen billowing into the sky must now be billowing directly overhead. He couldn't, in fact, see any distance at all.

In the smoke-grimed sky there were glowing firefly embers here and there. And he could make out little licks of flame at random spots in the paddock and in the trees. Just little licks of flame, nothing huge.

It all seemed to have happened very quickly, this change, this turn, but then perhaps he had in fact been unconscious for a few minutes after the roo had kicked him.

He turned back towards the car. The dogs were milling around behind the windows, swapping positions constantly, back and forwards, front window to back window, barking, although he could hardly hear them. He walked slowly, carefully back to the car, holding the balled-up shirt against his head. He opened the door, shooed the dogs into the back seat and climbed in. The dogs fussed about him, climbing between the seats and licking at him, barking. It took a moment to get them off him and bring them to order.

When he finally looked out the windscreen and along the road he saw more flying embers, more flames, little flames here and there, and he knew that he could no longer drive to the city. There was no massive front of fire ahead, but the embers had breached the ridge, which meant that there would be spot fires, and the spot fires would grow and would join together and would, he knew, become impassable. It would be madness to continue downhill now.

Images came to him, images of blackened cars with corpses in them that he had seen on news websites, and for just the slightest moment he felt as if the blackness behind him, the clog of smoke and looming unconsciousness, his unhappiness, teased him with a sense of calm, a sense that there was nowhere further he had to go, nothing further he had to do, a sense that this was where it all ended, and wasn't it surprising how ordinary it all was?

He felt at that moment the sum of everything he had ever done or been or said — through and through he was every single part of himself, every single moment — and at the same time he felt he was nothing.

His phone rang. It gave him a severe jolt, but he picked it up. There was a name on the screen: Ricky. Paul swiped his thumb over the screen — swiped right, answered the call.

'Where are you?' It was, of course, Ricky. Paul could tell he was using his serious, weighted, calm voice, but that it was a stretch for him.

'I don't know,' Paul said. 'On the road. In the car. With the chooks. Near the ridge — you know the ridge. Where are you?'

'I'm in Melbourne. The front has turned. You're blocked off. You should go home. It looks like it'll be safer back up our way.'

Home?

'Are you there? Do you hear me, Paul? Go home. Turn around and go home. Go home and turn the hoses on and stay inside. Just like we planned. Are you there?'

Go home? Why would he go back there? Back to those dishes in the sink, back to that same old married life lived like a Venn diagram, with he and Ricky only partly overlapping — the barest sliver of overlap. Why would he go back to that?

'Can you hear me?' the phone was asking. 'Go home. I'll be there as soon as I can get through.' And then: 'It'll be all right, Paul. You'll be all right.'

Paul had the shirt held over his right ear, clamping it on to the side of his head, but the left ear could hear fine.

'Yes,' he said, perversely responding to the third last thing Ricky had said. 'I can hear you. I'll turn around and go home.'

He turned on the ignition. After a few moments, Cher kicked in.

*

Paul remembered the first time he had seen Ricky at Three Faces —
he remembered it vividly. He was a fine featured young man, pretty
more so than handsome, slender rather than fit, with a wide generous
mouth and lovely teeth — a lovely smile. He seemed so animated,
laughing with his friends, and touching everyone as he spoke to them,
just gently, on the arm or the back. He seemed like the glue that stuck
the group together. Something about him made you want to know
him.

When the group washed up against the bar and, after a long time
spent sorting out orders and paying, Ricky had looked up and seen
Paul watching him, he had made a face at him, a sort of bug-eyed,
goony, grinning face, with a shrug of shoulders. It was so artless, it at
once acknowledged that he had noticed Paul watching, communicated
that he didn't mind, and invited Paul to join in their unbridled
enjoyment of the night. That look unravelled the usual cat's cradle of
cruising, looking, looking back, tentative advances, buying drinks, the
whole 1999 box and dice.

Paul would never normally have felt comfortable going up to
someone, especially not someone in a group of friends like that, but
something about that goony face-pulling made him feel invited, so he
did. Ricky had said hello as if he had known him for ages, made a silly
moue of a face, a different one this time, and at once taken Paul's arm,
leaned in very close to his ear and said in a crashing whisper: 'I'm
afraid I'm VERY pissed.'

Paul didn't really need to say anything; he was absorbed by the
group. One of them was even more pissed than Ricky, and there was a
lot of talk about whether or not he was going to pass out. Others were
being silly, talking in posh voices about it being only the 'shank of the
evening' or something. Paul didn't get any of it, but he just smiled and

let it flow over him, allowed himself to be held on to by Ricky, who occasionally lurched crazily away from him before tightening his grip, flexing his arm muscles and clinging tightly once more. Paul began to smile genuinely. It was all so silly.

'You drink the rest of this, will you?' Ricky asked at one point. 'I've had enough.' But then he immediately went on another expedition to the bar and bought another round.

At the end of the night, which had taken in two more clubs, more drinks, there was very little negotiating to be done about next steps. Paul and Ricky hailed a taxi in unison and said farewell to everyone milling around on the footpath. A few of the friends looked at Paul as if they didn't have a clue who he was, which was fair enough — he had that stolid uninteresting sort of face and body that blended in with the wallpaper. One friend, a girl — Liza this was; the first night he'd met her — kept asking Ricky if he would be all right, if he was sure he would be all right, while throwing covert dark looks at Paul as if trying to memorise his facial structure and hair and eye colour in case she had to Identikit him the following day.

They had gone back to Ricky's apartment, the one that would eventually become their second home, but they had been too drunk to fuck that first night. There was a lot of very slobbery kissing and falling all over furniture and then the bed, followed by some half-hard-dick sucking that didn't really achieve much. But before they could negotiate the fact that neither of them could get a hard-on and what that in fact left them with, they pretty much passed out.

The next day they discovered a shared kinship in their hangover. When they woke, groggy and muzzy-headed, they moved together but avoided direct mouth to mouth kisses. They both knew their breath was rank, but were too lazy to yet get out of bed and brush their teeth.

As a result, their interaction was somehow more tender than it might otherwise have been, turning their faces away, finding ears to kiss, a neck to nuzzle - a sort of coy, sleepy, amorous feeling enveloped them.

They revelled in the glorious out-of-control feeling of the sleep-wake cycle, one waking, wondering what the time was, hugging the other, nudging gently against him, then madly humping, nuzzling, kissing those out-of-the-way places, but then falling asleep again before seeing it through.

Eventually, long into the late afternoon, Paul woke to realise his dick was hard as a rock, so he slicked it with his own booze-rank spit, fingered Ricky's arse for a moment, then entered him without a condom, and they spoon-fucked until they fell asleep again without either of them achieving orgasm.

They drifted like this through their first day together, and formed a sort of heedless pheromone-driven bond that was never really broken. Many other things would come — reminding each other of their names for example — but when they properly awoke, actually got up and dressed and wandered downstairs to find something greasy to eat, they were amazed to find that the sun was setting, that there was a vivid pink sky, and that they were lovers.

THE PROPOSAL

Derek was immediately obvious as an outsider, a tourist, with his pale skin, and his slightly too intricate backpack with toggles and zips and the suggestion of hidden compartments for passport and cash and cards — his air somewhere between befuddlement and determination. But there were many tourists here in Jordan, and they were all traipsing around in the heat, groups and couples mostly, all looking equally befuddled and determined. And hot. What was different about him was that he was alone.

He had a pre-booked and pre-paid three-day tour from Amman to Petra, Wadi Rum, the Dead Sea, and back to Amman. He was meant to be doing it with his boyfriend, Chris, but Chris had not come with him from London to Amman and so he was doing it alone.

They had been travelling through the UK together for the last three weeks and had spent their time almost equally divided between going out with Chris's old friends and travelling to rather grim areas of Greater London for meals with Chris's extended family. Chris had grown up in the UK, emigrating to Australia with his dad's family when he was in his mid-teens. His mum and stepdad still lived in the UK.

They had done very little themselves as a twosome, apart from that one night in London, the night before they were due to fly out. The idea had been that they would fly from London Heathrow to Amman in Jordan and do the tour, hang out for a bit in Amman, and then go home to Melbourne. They liked the idea of getting out into the clear warm desert after the chilly civilisation of the UK. But then — well, then things hadn't gone precisely to plan and Derek had ended up making the flight to Amman by himself.

Derek had been overseas many times, but even he would not call himself a seasoned traveller. He had been on family holidays when he was young, Bali with a group after graduation, and he had been on many overseas trips with Chris. Chris was a much more experienced traveller than him. He took control of the bookings, the tickets, the currency, the itineraries. He set alarms for when they needed to get up, carried sleeping pills for when they needed to zonk out on the planes, supplied Eno for upset bellies and Rescue Remedy for stress. He spoke Spanish semi-fluently and could get by with tourist German and French. He had friends and family in the UK and in a smattering of other European countries. Derek spoke only English and knew nobody outside Australia other than the people Chris had introduced him to. He had never travelled by himself before.

Even so, when he went on to Amman by himself, following the itinerary that Chris had prepared, he didn't feel it was a brave or unusual thing to do. He didn't think it was foolish either. Chris had booked and paid for everything, the tickets the accommodation, the tour — it didn't occur to him not to go. But the moment he walked out of the airport into that clear warm air — hotter than he had imagined — he wondered whether he would manage it by himself.

They had not arranged a driver or researched any other way to get them from the airport to central Amman. They had just trusted to being able to work it out together when they got there. Luckily, perhaps, almost immediately everything was taken out of Derek's hands. When he exited the airport a young Arab boy began walking along beside him, asking if he needed a taxi, pointing in the direction of the taxi rank, and trying to take his case all at the one time. The boy was at once ingratiating, deferential, and insistent. Derek felt a twinge of unease, but, as the taxi rank did indeed seem like the only place to get a taxi, he let the boy lead him there, although he did retain possession of his case.

Once he got there a number of men jumped up from where they were lounging along the gutter. There seemed to be a boss, who shooed the boy away and gave a chit of paper to one of the men. This man then gestured to the back of the rank and Derek followed him there. When they arrived at the car it did not appear to be a taxi at all, but a private car — grey and slightly old. But the driver had already put his case in the boot and was cheerfully indicating the passenger side door. He appeared to speak no English whatsoever.

Derek, feeling that it would take more effort to extricate himself from the situation than it would to go along with it, decided to let himself be taken for a ride. The driver was cheerful and appeared to know the address when Derek said it. Everything seemed very normal and above board.

The highway into town, a three-lane carriageway, was in atrocious condition, broken up into small rocks of bitumen and dirt in some places. The driver — Derek never got his name — tail-gated other cars and trucks to within an inch, feathering on the brake and accelerator to keep as close as possible. When he wasn't doing this he was overtaking, although mostly he straddled lanes when he did so, squeezing between trucks and cars and hurtling forward at a great speed. While doing this he was also using his mobile phone to translate different messages for Derek. He would speak in Arabic into his phone, then he would hold it up to Derek and let the phone translate the phrase into English in a slightly robotic tone.

'Welcome to a man,' the robotic voice said.

Derek, who was stomping on an imaginary footbrake on the passenger-side floor every few seconds, was charmed and amused.

'Thank you,' he said. Then, wondering if the driver understood even this small bit of English, nodded and smiled broadly in dumb show.

'How do you like a man?' the phone asked next.

Derek smiled again. He liked a man in various ways.

He began to feel a smidgeon more comfortable with the driver and the tailgating and the decidedly odd overtaking method. No-one else, not the driver, not the other drivers of the other cars, seemed to see anything odd about it.

'It's beautiful,' Derek said to the driver, answering the phone translated question, but then remembering that the driver didn't speak English he made an expansive gesture to the pale rocky ground that stretched out all around them, with concrete block houses scattered across the landscape, a good fifty percent of them half-built, and with the air of being abandoned. He gestured and nodded and smiled. 'I feel like the Queen Mother,' he thought to himself.

'Are you married?' the phone translated next.

Was he married? Was that another mistranslation or not?

'No,' he said, shaking his head, a little bewildered.

The driver moved one hand off the wheel and cupped his crotch, looking at Derek in a suggestive way. Some things didn't need Google Translate. Derek shook his head briefly and turned to look out at the rocky terrain. It was not really beautiful at all, he felt. It was in fact quite grim.

It was Chris who mentioned marriage first. It had been back in 2017, the year of the same-sex marriage vote in Australia. Derek had been dreaming. He was in a field of lush green grass. He was lying down on his stomach, and the grass was ticklish against his cheek. The earth was warm and soft under him, like their mattress, and he could feel the sun on his back through his pyjamas, and on the back of his neck. He had an erection, a thoughtless morning-wood kind of erection which leant the scenario a warm, lazy eroticism that it didn't otherwise deserve. It was, after all, just a field of grass.

'We should get married,' Chris had said.

Derek wasn't sure whether Chris spoke from the grassy field or from the pillow beside him. He didn't respond.

'Are you awake?'

Derek made a noise into the pillow.

'I think we should get married.'

Derek woke up more fully. The warm grass and the erection receded. He half rolled over and cracked open an eye. Chris, a morning person, looked perky and bright.

'What? What are you …' his sentence remained unfinished.

'We — should — get — married.' Chris said each word clearly.

'Mmm. Can we talk about it later?'

Chris and Derek had been together for roughly eight years when there was the vote on same-sex marriage in Australia. They had campaigned for marriage equality, marched on Parliament holding a

LOVE IS LOVE and an EQUALITY IS A RIGHT sign, gone together to the Australia Post red letterbox down the end of their street and posted their votes in the marriage equality survey, each of them taking a photo of the other with their envelope half in half out of the letterbox. A week after the result of the survey was announced, in a mood of relief and exhilaration, Chris had blurted out his pillow proposal, and after that they had, pretty much, been engaged to be married.

*

After being delivered to the villa by the taxi that didn't seem to be a taxi, Derek had a snooze, a shower, and then wandered out into the streets looking for food. Almost instantly he felt completely out of his comfort zone. Why were so many men looking at him? Was he looking back too much? He walked on, telling himself not to be so self-conscious.

Homosexuality was not illegal in Jordan — theoretically. Chris had done all the research on this before arranging the trip. While not illegal, it was also socially frowned upon, and, he had told Derek, gay people may find themselves the target of vilification if they are too overt in public. In fact, gay couples had been known to be arrested for public displays of affection. It was best, then, to be discreet. This didn't bother Derek terribly much. He hadn't expected he and Chris would be snogging on the streets, and as far as he was aware he didn't look particularly gay. He took no pains to be straight-acting, certainly, but he was a solid, not-particularly handsome fellow, and there wasn't much gay-acting about him either. He was, anyhow, the sort of person others would look past without wondering about his sexuality. Or, at least, it had been that way in Australia and in the UK. But in the Middle East, in Jordan, things seemed to be different. For some reason people did look at him here. Men, especially — well it was mostly men you saw, in the streets, in taxis, in shops. They all seemed to be looking at him.

Derek found a deli and bought some supplies, then ducked into a nearby bottle shop.

The man behind the counter looked at him long and hard before asking where he was from.

'Australia.'

'Ahh. Kangaroos.'

'Yes. Just these thanks.' Derek put a couple of beers on the counter.

'Are you married?'

That same question again. And no chance of a mistranslation this time.

'No,' Derek said, more puzzled than offended.

'Do you have a girlfriend?'

Derek said no, and the man grinned.

'I like you,' he said. 'You come back.'

Derek hurried back to the villa where he spent the night in with his snacks, his beer, and the call to prayer blasting across the terrace from a nearby mosque.

Sammi, the driver that Chris had arranged for them, texted him to confirm a pick-up time for the next morning. After a moment of indecision, during which he considered cancelling the whole thing, Derek texted back a time. He did it partly because he was a little tipsy, and confident with it, and partly because if he didn't go on the pre-arranged tour, what would he do?

After that, Derek thought briefly about going out to the one gay bar (known about by his travel guide) in Amman, which was conveniently just around the corner from the villa, but while he was tipsy enough to consider it he wasn't drunk enough to brave it.

*

He found Petra difficult. Yes, there it was, all that red rock with caves and carved facades. A remarkable achievement and all that, a wonder of the ancient world, but it left him feeling unimpressed, and he found himself not enjoying it very much. It was being alone that did it. Of course he wasn't actually alone. There were scores of tourists, and every step of the way, literally on the steps up to the high temple and the high place of sacrifice, there was someone trying to sell him something. With Chris this would have meant something — alone it meant very little. The continued propositions didn't help.

The donkey boy at Petra was a remarkable looking young man with braided hair and kohl around his eyes, who walked behind Derek on the donkey as they descended through the amazing cliffs into the city of Petra.

'I like what I see,' he said.

'What?' Derek asked.

'Mmmmm. Yeah. I like what I see.' And then, 'Are you married?'

'No,' Derek said, his heart sinking.

The man went on, saying such dirty things about what he would like to do to Derek and how strong and 'plump' his arse was, that Derek was appalled and amazed at the same time. He tried to take it with amused tolerance, tried to imagine making a funny story out of how often he was being propositioned, but he could no longer imagine telling these stories — certainly not to Chris. In any case, it was starting to wear thin. It was no longer so amusing. Perhaps, at a distance, he might find it amusing, make an amusing story from it, but here and now it was starting to feel something akin to persecution.

The most overt proposition, as it turned out, was from a taxi driver in Petra. The one from the airport had been nothing compared to the driver who picked him up at the gates of Petra to take him back up the hill to his hotel. Within the space of a couple of minutes the conversation had gone from zero to breakneck.

'Are you married?' the driver asked as soon as he had climbed in the car and they arranged the destination. He was a compact little man with a round belly, tight-looking against his polo shirt, a moustache and the big, direct, brown eyes Derek had seen many times already.

'No,' Derek said, stiffening slightly.

'Why not?' he asked

'No reason,' Derek said.

'Are you gay?' the driver asked.

Derek paused for a moment.

'Yes,' he said. He looked up the hill and tried to find a building that was familiar. If he could get his bearings, he could get out of the taxi if he needed to, and just walk the rest of the way.

'I'm gay too,' the driver said with amazement. 'We can have sex.' It was half a question, half a statement — actually more of a statement.

'No,' Derek said calmly.

The driver put his hand on Derek's leg and squeezed, then as Derek swatted it away, the man brought his hand up and tweaked Derek's nipple through his teeshirt. Derek flinched away and brushed the hand off. It had been an expert tweak. No groping about. Hit it right on the bullseye immediately. The squeeze was hard — a definite pinch.

Derek was embarrassed, but more because of how out of shape he was. As the man grabbed his nipple, Derek was more aware of how floppy his pec was — almost man-boobs — than anything else. He kept his eye on the hilltop, trying to find his bearings.

Oddly, he didn't feel offended. There was no way he was going to do anything with this man — he was in a strange country and he wasn't sufficiently horny or attracted to the compact little tit-pincher to risk it. But he wasn't offended by it. He didn't want a scene. He merely wanted to get back to the hotel and back to his room.

'Would you like to look at my dick?' the driver asked.

'No, thank you,' Derek said primly.

'You just have to look at it.'

The man was so matter of fact, so unswerving in his intention, that Derek, for the briefest moment, contemplated agreeing to look at his dick in order to avoid a scene, before he saw a building on the hill ahead of them that he recognised as the hotel. It was very close.

'Just drop me here would be fine,' he said.

He paid — the driver asked a lot more than the short distance warranted, but Derek was by now used to the wildly fluctuating prices, and inured to being ripped off — and walked the rest of the way.

Back in his hotel room, a room with a cool tiled floor and a heavily curtained window, he locked the door, had a long shower, turned the light off and lay naked on the sheets.

*

It had been Chris's idea, the pact. Depending on who you asked, it was either a grand romantic gesture or embarrassingly twee. Derek was not a romantic at heart, as was universally known amongst their friends, and when the pact was announced at their farewell before the trip, he was very clearly on the eye-rolling side of the fence, albeit in a good natured, jokey fashion. 'The rules of the engagement,' Chris called it, and everyone had a good laugh at the whole scenario, painting Chris as the romantic and Derek as curmudgeonly but secretly loving it. Chris, perhaps predictably, as it was his idea, was gung-ho about the whole thing.

It had started when they had gone to pick up their engagement rings. They were simple rings, engraved on the inside with their initials, but when the finished products were in their hands, the boxes popped open, Chris had demurred at them actually putting the rings on. It didn't feel, he said, like they'd got properly engaged.

'What do you mean?'

'Well, I didn't ask you — not properly. And you haven't asked me.'

'I don't care,' Derek had said. The wrong thing to say, of course.

'You don't care?'

'I mean I don't *mind*.'

There followed a conversation that to Derek felt interminably long and round-about. But the upshot was the pact, and the pact was this: between the moment they left the ground in Melbourne and the moment they touched down again, each of them would have to propose, in any way, shape or form they liked, separately, to the other, and be accepted, before they could be considered truly engaged to be married. And so they had taken off on their trip to the UK and Jordon, with each other's ring in its own little silk-lined, felt-covered box in their luggage.

Chris had been the first to propose. He had done it at a family dinner, a grand affair with his extended UK family, including his mum and dad, soon after they had touched down. He had gone down on one knee, he had proposed, he had popped open the box and taken out the ring. Derek had said yes. What else could he say in that circumstance?

The short and not so sweet truth was that Derek was more and more sure that he didn't in fact want to marry Chris. He liked Chris a lot, and he liked living with Chris, liked sleeping with him and waking up with him, he liked being with Chris, travelling with Chris — he was an easy person to be with. Did he love Chris? He didn't think about love very much, and didn't much believe in it — well, not in a big romantic swooning kind of way. But then again, maybe love was indeed what they had — tenderness, a sense of comfort and knowledge of the other, born from the cumulative effect of days and years spent together. Maybe that was all love was? If so, then yes, Derek loved Chris. But even so, the idea of marriage left him feeling cold.

If he thought about it — and he had thought about it, a lot, especially after the advent of the pact — the coolness was because he had never really chosen to be with Chris. He'd said yes when Chris had asked him out. He'd put out when Chris had put the moves on him. He'd agreed to move in. In time, he'd agreed to a joint bank account and a mortgage. Why not? There was no reason not to. He had been a willing participant all the way, happily going along with Chris all down the line. And then one day he'd woken up and he'd looked at himself, at his life, with a strange sense of bewilderment and distance, and thought: *I didn't choose any of this.*

Their last night together in London, after a West End show followed by supper and drinks, they had ended up on the Tube, buoyed by a good night out, slightly tipsy. The train had taken off with a jerk before they had taken their seat, and they fell on their bottoms heavily, virtually on top of each other. Chris, taking advantage of the proximity, had given Derek a quick stage-kiss, a big showy smackeroo, and they'd laughed and felt a rush of bonhomie. Chris had looked at Derek, seemed about to say something, then thought better of it and sat back in his seat, his eyes wide and expectant, a demure little smirk on his lips.

'He's waiting for me to propose,' Derek thought. He noticed that Chris had even moved his feet slightly to one side in case he, Derek, took it into his mind to take advantage of their 'moment' and go down on one knee right there on the floor of the carriage.

It was, after all, his turn.

*

Sammi picked up Derek at the Petra hotel at 7am, an early start for a long drive to Wadi Rum, where he would spend the day.

Sammi did not ask him if he was married. Sammi did not proposition him. Sammi drove. Sammi smoked. Sammi hummed along to the radio. Sammi was a big, smiling man, but totally uninterested in his passenger.

It was, of course, meant to be the two of them, Derek and Chris, and a driver of their own had not seemed like a ridiculous idea when it was the two of them. By himself Derek did, at first, feel slightly ridiculous, but he soon got over it. The roads were long and straight, and although the car was air-conditioned, it was too hot for self-doubt out here on the rocky plains of Jordan.

In the UK Derek had done all the driving in the rental, and had a rough idea of where they were and what direction they were travelling in at all times. Here in Jordan he had no idea — he was completely in the hands of others, the drivers, the tour guides, the taxi drivers.

Going from Petra to Wadi Rum he found himself completely disoriented. He knew nothing other than that they were driving across the desert in what seemed to be roughly the one direction.

When they arrived at the Tourist Information Centre at Wadi Rum, Sammi went and took care of the tickets while Derek got his things together. The Centre was an ugly square concrete building with Arabic writing on the façade and an English translation underneath. The carpark was large but cars were only sparsely parked. It did not seem to be a busy day at Wadi Rum.

When Sammi came back he brought a very slender young Arab man wearing full length white robes buttoned up at the neck and the wrists, and a red and white keffiyeh on his head.

'This is Hossein,' Sammi said to Derek.

Derek said hello, and Hossein greeted him with a nod and a smile. He had a fine-boned face with a large quite majestic nose, brown eyes with thick eyelashes. When he smiled he had very big and very white teeth.

'Hossein is your driver today,' Sammi said.

'Another one?' Derek was just about done with drivers.

'Yes. He's very good. You go with him.'

Hossein half nodded half bowed to Sammi, who had been quite peremptory with him, as if to a servant, turned and indicated that Derek should follow. Hossein sauntered away — scuffed his feet along in large padded sandals, and swiped his fingertips towards anything remotely close-by as he walked — a car, or a wall — without quite touching anything. To Derek, following behind, he seemed like a teenager slouching along, purposefully slow, so he could be late to school.

At the far end of the carpark there were a number of Nissan tray-trucks, all a little beat up, with the two seater cab up front, and the tray rigged up with two bench seats running length-wise either side of the tray, and a canopy above in canvas striped red and orange and yellow, with a fringing of gold. It all looked like it had been left in the sun a little too long, and perhaps done one or two tourist seasons too many.

There were other young men there, in white robes and the red and white keffiyeh — a uniform, presumably, that they wore for the tourists. There were a couple of older men, but they wore regular clothes, slacks and button-up shirts and appeared to be in charge of the herd of more traditionally dressed young men.

Hossein moseyed to the cab of one of the tray trucks and came back to Derek with a one litre bottle of water. It was ice-cold.

'You get up,' Hossein said — again, it was less of a question than a statement — no-one seemed to properly ask questions in Jordan.

Derek did as he was told, stowed the water in a small strip of shade under the seat, and soon they were off through the village of Wadi Rum, a ramshackle little place with a lot of speed-humps. Derek felt every single one of them. Then the bitumen road simply ended. They passed out of the town and were instantly in the desert.

Derek gripped the side of the tray truck and stared in awe.

Red sand, miles of red sand, with rocky outcrops, mountains actually, which seemed to rise almost vertically, flat topped, from the sand. It had the simplicity of a painted backdrop, or a constructed landscape — flat sand, vertical squares of rock, and the entire sky the same flat blue. But what he loved most was that it seemed utterly empty. There, in front of him, he could only see a couple of other tray trucks, like his own, presumably with other tourists in them, but they must have been miles away, cutting across the red sand in different directions.

Since arriving in Jordan he had felt observed, singled out, harried to some degree or other. Petra had been full of tourists all jostling to see the same thing, take the same photo, and just as full of locals, all trying to sell him donkey rides, camel rides, carved animals, sweet tea, cans of Coke, pieces of red rock. In Amman he had felt watched from the moment he stepped out of the villa, monitored as he walked down the street. He had been hailed, cajoled into shops or restaurants with the promise of sweet tea at no cost, welcomed, vaunted, flirted with, propositioned, but everywhere it seemed to him that smiling welcome could turn to recrimination in the moment it took to step past.

But now, in Wadi Rum, here he was, just him, alone. Well, Hossein was there, but he was hidden in the cab up front. Derek could only see the back of the keffiyeh if he bobbed down and looked through the small back window. He finally felt as if he was driving away from the people, the commerce, the propositions, the sweet tea — he felt as if he was finally seeing the land itself. And it felt wonderful.

At that moment, Hossein stomped his sandalled foot onto the accelerator. They sped off over the desert sand, and Derek felt a surprisingly fresh breeze in his face, dry but clean, peeling off over his sunburnt nose and cooling his sweat-soaked temples. The mountains moved slightly as they drove across the sand, as if rearranging themselves like backdrop flats on a stage, one shouldering aside another.

After about ten minutes they came to a stop alongside a couple of other tray trucks lined up alongside a large square tent, a rudimentary parking lot at the base of one of the rocky outcrops.

The rock was large, about as big as a city block at the base, maybe, but not as massive as the mountains themselves ranging along the horizon. The outcrop consisted of odd shaped boulders of red rock, much the same as the colour of the rock at Petra, with a scree of rocks and stones and sand in the gaps and chasms between. On one side of the outcrop, the red sand of the dessert had piled up like a great dune. The sand was bright red and there were divots in the side of it as if people had earlier walked up, but the wind had smoothed out their footsteps.

Obviously something about the way the wind travelled through this great arena between the mountains, carried grains of sand in just such a way that they piled up against the side of this outcrop but nowhere else.

Hossein appeared from the front of the cabin as Derek dropped out of the tray and stood looking at the dune. Two figures appeared at the top of the rock. Derek was surprised how small they seemed. It was bigger than he had supposed.

'They film many things here,' Hossein said, in a bored kind of way, gesturing at the dune. '*Star Wars. Lawrence of Arabia.* And *The Martian* with Matt Damon.'

Hossein squinted at the dune for a bit, giving Derek time to take it all in.

'You climb,' he then said. It was, again, more of a statement than a question. Hossein was suggesting he climb, but it sounded like an order. 'I wait here.' He pointed to the tent.

'Okay,' Derek said, and stepped off towards the dune obediently. The sand was warm and loose and his feet sank to his ankles and slipped back every step of the way. He tried a laboured run for a few steps, but that did nothing but churn more sand out behind him. He would not make it up the dune this way. He stopped and looked up.

Two other figures appeared at the top of the dune, laughing and cajoling each other to go down first. Derek moved sideways across the surface of the dune to the rocky edge, found firmer footing and began very slowly picking his way up the side of the rock along the edge of the sand. He stopped to watch the others, two young men in cut off shorts and football jerseys, both with NY caps and dark glasses on, as they ran down the length of the dune, kicking up wheels of sand and shouting and laughing. One of them fell, perhaps purposefully, and rolled down past his friend, trying to catch at his legs and trip him over. Derek's lips moved in the smallest smile. It was such cute horseplay. He wondered if they were a couple. But then he saw two others, two girls of around the same age, come down the dune more carefully, holding hands to steady themselves. Their girlfriends, probably. He turned and continued on to the top of the rock.

It was flat-topped, as all the mountains appeared to be, and about the size of a football field. He lifted his hat off his head and held his elbows out, so that the breeze blew under his arms, and across the top of his head. It was that same desert breeze, dry, neither warm nor cool, but refreshing when it touched hot skin or sweat soaked temples.

He turned slowly in a circle, taking in the surroundings. The far-off village of Wadi Rum itself, the massive flat-topped mountains dotted around the entire horizon, and there, down on the red sands — was it? Yes it was — camels crossing the desert single file. They were so small in the distance, just mini camel-shaped silhouettes, but as he watched he could see the way they moved, that loping undulating walk they had. And those other dots, slightly smaller, squarer, faster - they were other tray trucks, speeding across the sands in different directions, taking other tourists to other rocks and dunes, presumably.

It was all so much larger than he thought, this arena of sand and rock and dunes. And he was so much further away from everything than he thought, standing on a rock in the middle of a desert, seeing miniature silhouettes of camels undulating through the heat haze in the distance. How far away from your life, your habits, everything you knew, did you have to be for it to not belong to you any longer?

He began to feel a sense of lightness. A sense of emptiness, even. It was a peaceful feeling, comforting — his breath came more easily, the breeze cooled him — and yet it was also slightly unnerving, being so far away from everything he knew, being so far away and being there alone.

When Derek got to the bottom of the dune — it was so much easier stomp-sliding down than it was going up — Hossein was there, waiting in the shade of the 4WD.

'We go,' Hossein said.

'Just a minute,' Derek said. 'I have to get the sand out of my shoes.' He sat on the back edge of the tray truck and started undoing his shoes.

Hossein watched as Derek took his shoe off and poured a stream of sand out.

'All the tourists wear shoes,' he said, in a tone disapproving and slightly bewildered. He poked one of his feet out from the bottom of his white robe, kicked off one of his wide padded sandals, then pointed his toe at it as if indicating the correct sort of footwear to Derek. He had smooth-skinned feet, well-shaped and surprisingly clean. They were the feet of a boy. Derek looked at the foot and then at Hossein. Hossein smiled at him. He had brown eyes, and it was difficult to see where the iris stopped and the pupil started — they were large and uniformly dark.

He found himself wondering how old Hossein was. He seemed very young, but was obviously old enough to drive. Although that didn't mean a thing, really, as Derek didn't know how old you had to be to get a licence in Jordan. He didn't even know if the kid did have a licence. Hossein, for his part, seemed unembarrassed by the slightly prolonged eye-contact.

'We go,' Hossein said again, then dropped his eyes, scuffed his foot back into his sandal, and headed to the driver's side of the truck.

Soon they were off over the desert again, driving further and further away from the village, across the sand. The mountains again moved, shouldering in and out of each other's way. After fifteen or so minutes — it was hard to tell, Derek didn't wear a watch, and wasn't really paying attention to the time on his phone — they again stopped. This time they were at a smaller rock formation at the base of one of the mountains. It was a twist of red rock, like a pretzel or something, creating an arch that was not big enough to drive through but big enough to walk through.

There was another tent here, much like the one at the dune, but this time there were no other cars parked there. They were there alone.

Hossein climbed out of the cab and came to the back of the truck.

'You climb,' he said.

'You want me to climb up to the top of the arch?'

'Up the side there. You see the steps. For your foot.'

Derek saw rudimentary steps carved out of the rock creating a sort of stairway to the top of the arch. It didn't look that hard.

'You give me your phone,' Hossein demanded.

'What?'

'Your phone. I take photo.'

Derek did as he was asked, unlocking and handing over his phone to Hossein who promptly turned away and went into the tent where it was shady. He only came out of the tent when Derek had, sweating and puffing, made it to the top of the arch. Hossein moved into position down on the sand and held up Derek's phone.

'Jump,' Hossein shouted from down on the ground.

What? Jump off? There was no way Derek was going to jump off the arch down onto the sand. No way. It was much too high.

'You jump,' Hossein said again, as insistent as ever.

Perhaps this is what all the tourists did. Perhaps it was such a soft landing in the sand that it wasn't dangerous. But no — surely not. It was such a long way down. Although maybe it wasn't as far as it looked. Everything out here in the desert seemed so much further away than perhaps in reality it was. Derek took a tentative step forward.

'Jump,' Hossein said for a third time, and this time he demonstrated what he meant, doing a star jump in the air.

Derek stepped back and did a star-jump while Hossein took photos. Hossein then returned to the tent, leaving Derek to lower himself slowly and awkwardly, bum in the air, down the rock stairs.

After the arch they continued, driving further away from Wadi Rum village, randomly it seemed to Derek, across the desert. It was difficult to tell which direction they drove in, and in fact sometimes it seemed they were driving in large arcs, rather than in a straight line. There seemed to be an endless supply of sand and mountains-on-the-horizon.

They always seemed to be following a track of sorts, made up of the wheel-marks of other 4WDs, and sometimes they would break off one track and join another, rocketing over the edges of the tyre-marks like one boat breaking across the wake of another.

Further and further away. But also on the way towards something, somewhere. He could feel it. On the way somewhere. Where was Hossein taking him?

Their next stop was at a chasm in one of the cliffs in which there was an ancient carving of stick figure men and a fire. After that they drove to another rock, with a large cave halfway up where, Hossein told him, Lawrence of Arabia had apparently slept. The routine at these two spots had been the same. They stopped, Hossein would say, 'You climb' and then retreat to the shade while Derek, the mad pale white guy, did as he was told and scaled rocks in the almost-midday sun. They only saw one other 4WD between these two sites, and only at the chasm were there other people.

Derek had been having a lot of water, and the climbs had only been slightly arduous, but even so he was getting hot and tired and even a little light-headed. He was also completely sick of hearing about Lawrence of Arabia. For these reasons, at the next stop, another where there was a tent and no-one else in evidence, when Hossein climbed out of the cab and said, 'You climb,' Derek said, 'No.'

Hossein looked at Derek wide-eyed — it was a look of shock and apprehension.

'You not okay.' A question and not a question.

'I'm fine.'

'I have more water for you.'

'I've got plenty. I'm fine.'

'You not climb.'

'No. I'm done with climbing. I'm going to just sit in the shade with you. Relax.'

Hossein smiled and nodded. He was relieved.

'Come,' he said, and he indicated the way to the tent. Inside the tent was unexpectedly lavish. It was fully carpeted on the floor, the walls and the ceiling, with traditional rugs of mainly red and gold, with long sausages of cushion around each of the walls. Hossein indicated a spot on the floor for Derek, then squatted and reclined to one side, landing with his elbow on one of the cushions, the rest of him in a comfortable pose across the floor. He was instantly at ease and utterly relaxed. Derek, on the other hand, never comfortable on the floor, squatted awkwardly and sat on the cushion as if it was a low chair. He found Hossein's lithe abandonment on the floor beside him suggestive, but he couldn't decide whether it was unselfconsciously so or not.

'You from Australia,' Hossein stated.

'Yes, that's right,' Derek said.

'I would like to go to Australia.'

'You've never been?'

'No.'

'Have you travelled at all?'

'I've never been, no.'

'Anywhere?'

'No. I live at the village. I work every day.'

'Every day?'

'During the tourist season, every day. Other times, not at all.'

'I see,' Derek said.

The air in the tent was stuffy, but it was not uncomfortable. They were both looking out the open flap of the tent, where a triangle of red sand showed long and hot into the distance. They spoke slowly, with long pauses between their sentences.

'You like photo?' Hossein eventually asked.

'My photo?'

'From the arch.'

'Oh, the ones you took? I didn't look yet.' Derek unlocked his phone and called up his photo stream. He swiped back through his photos — so many photos of red sand and red rock — would he ever even look at them again? He had scrolled too far, so stopped and started swiping forward slowly. There was the dune, the view of the camels from the top of the rock, more sand, more rock, and then, there he was standing on top of the arch of rock. At first he was just standing there, but then, as the photos progressed — Hossein had taken an awful lot of photos — he had his arms up, and then, yes, there was one with him doing the most awkward half-hearted star jump that had ever been done before.

He laughed.

He felt happy.

He had gone far enough away, from everything, from himself, that some tie had been severed and he didn't actually have to go back. *He didn't have to go back.*

He was still lazily swiping forward, without really looking. The photos of him doing a star jump were followed by photos of the interior of a tent, much the same as the one they were now in, but presumably the tent at the arch. This was followed by Hossein's own dainty feet in those sandals, a white covered knee up close and out of focus — presumably a mistake those two — and then, staring back at him, a series of selfies, of Hossein himself, with his dark eyes and gaze at once bold and innocent, leering, poking his tongue out, and then merely smiling, every selfie, to Derek, dripping with fresh sexual threat — not promise or possibility, but threat.

Derek showed the screen to Hossein. He smirked and smothered a smile.

'You don't mind.' Again, a question without the correct inflection of a question.

'I don't mind. I'm glad to have the pictures.'

Derek felt as if he was utterly in Hossein's hands, here at the end of the earth, in a tent with carpets on the floor and the walls and the ceiling. I am adrift, he thought, a million miles away from my life. I am nothing but promise. I am nothing but possibility. I am in your hands.

Hossein looked at him, a mixture of business-like and friendly, aloof and conspiratorial, innocent and wicked. The question, when it came, was expected, although, of course, it didn't really sound like a question.

'You are married,' Hossein said.

Derek smiled.

'No,' he said.

'Why not?'

Derek shook his head. He remembered that last night in London. It had ended the way all of their other joint decisions had unfolded — Chris had done all the running, Derek had merely acquiesced. It was later the night of the Tube kiss. They'd got back to their hotel room and shrugged off their coats, kicked off their shoes, taken off their pants. At this crossroad where it could have gone one way, it went another, and Derek began to get ready for bed — pottering around, folding clothes, cleaning his teeth. Chris came and leaned on the bathroom doorframe.

'You're not going to propose, are you?' he asked.

'No,' Derek said. 'I'm sorry, but I'm not.'

And now here was Hossein asking him why. He didn't know what to say.

'Don't need,' Hossein said, smiling, innocent — a question but not a question.

Derek began to smile.

'No,' he agreed. 'Don't need.'

ELEPHANT

Dr Robert and JD were driving to Mount Elephant together in the doctor's silver BMW coupe. It was the end of summer, and the western plains of Victoria, vast and flat as a tack, except for the mounds of extinct volcanoes here and there, were dry and beige-coloured as far as the eye could see. It had been an uneventful drive, apart from the ten minutes or so that JD masturbated and filmed it on his iPhone.

Dr Robert watched JD doing this as often as he judged it safe to turn his head, but as the roads were long and flat and he could see oncoming traffic for miles before it got anywhere near them, he managed to see quite a bit. He'd seen JD's dick before, of course — many times, both in online videos and up close and personal, but there was something so uncanny about the size of it, that it was almost impossible not to look. It didn't seem real. It was like CGI. It was like a ride at Dreamworld. It was like fireworks. It was like childbirth (he had been an obstetrician). It was uncanny and beautiful and gobsmacking — every single time.

JD's full name was Jose Diego Romero Benitez, he was 27, he was born in Brazil but based in London. He had traditional Brazilian-bombshell looks — tan skin, dark hair, thick rosy lips and big dark eyes. His body was as muscled and tight as the gym could make it, his

nipples were dark and chunky, and his dick was preternaturally large —
somewhere between miraculous and ridiculous.

JD had 430k followers on Twitter and 775k on Instagram, and he
regularly posted semi-nude selfies on both.

'Is a fine line,' he had explained to Dr Robert soon after they met,
as if he was explaining something really intricate and tricky. 'For
Instagram is behind cloth only, either in underwear or behind a towel.
Nothing sheer. And is got to be pointing down.'

'I see,' Dr Robert nodded, utterly besotted. 'Pointing down.'

'Yeah. It can be, like, pretty much hard, but as long as is pointing
down is fine.'

'Okay.'

'On Twitter you can get away with a lot more. Facebook?' He
made a sound something like a Brazilian version of 'pfft'. 'I do not
bother with Facebook.'

JD had wank videos behind a paywall on his own website, which
Dr Robert had seen many of, and teaser trailers on most of the other
free porn video hosting sites, where he could post pretty much
whatever he wanted. He was, world-wide-web-wise, everywhere, and
determined to crack his first million followers by the end of the year.

In his online bio he described himself as an entrepreneur (he had a
range of underwear, which of course he modelled extensively himself);
a dancer (he was regularly booked at clubs around Europe and South
America as a podium dancer slash stripper); and a 'citizen of the
world'. He was also what is, in the social media circus, known as 'an
influencer'. He received payment to promote all manner of goods, but
mostly those that could be shown to advantage alongside a monster-
cock — primarily underwear, but also workout gear, caps, gym

supplements, gym shoes, bow ties, and, rather oddly, a high-end range of eye glasses. He had 20/20 vision.

Dr Robert had met JD after one of his appearances at a club in Brazil, and one thing having led to the traditional other, Dr Robert had brought him back to Australia and installed him in the guest bedroom for an extended holiday.

Strictly speaking, they weren't a couple, it was too uneven a match for that, but they had an arrangement that suited them both. If JD was aware of the terms of the arrangement a little more than Dr Robert, then that would be because he had experienced many more arrangements of this kind in the past. Dr Robert was, in comparison, a bit more of a hopeless romantic. If really pressed he might say that, yes, he did believe that one day his prince would come, and so what if this prince turned out to be less than half his age and a seriously stacked Brazilian 'social influencer'.

For his part, JD adhered to the rules he had in his own head about what was going on with Dr Robert. When Dr Robert and he were out together he paid him a rather lofty, offhand attention, and studiously ignored everyone else — the way he stared across the room over everyone's heads was, if not quite convincing, at least fulfilling his part of the deal. On the other hand, when Dr Robert wasn't around, he felt free to do as he pleased, and he was currently pleasing himself with a couple of guys from a gym he'd been going to since he arrived in town.

In return for sex, and for this public show of exclusive attention, JD extracted gifts and cash from Dr Robert — a 'loan' of some odd thousands to help pay off a pesky debt he had back home, some money for new clothes, the crocodile-embossed low-rise sneakers for example, which cost $915, a flight to Sydney for a party he wanted to attend to make some money to pay back the 'loan', and so on. These gifts were expertly calibrated in JDs head to be adequate as payment without seeming like payment. Whether Dr Robert was aware of this fine distinction JD didn't know and didn't really care.

JD made his living, if you could call it that, from his penis — his face, his youth and his muscles, certainly, but his penis mostly. He made a better living than most people in 9 to 5 jobs. And every day, in order to provide his various online platforms with the content required, he would get himself half-hard and, dick pointing down, underwear in place, take a number of selfies, with or without sponsored items on his person. He would also, once a day, once every single day, jerk off, film it and post it online. His website was called thedailyJD.com.

This explains why, one bare foot up on the dash, his singlet pulled up and over his head to reveal his pecs and his abs, and his dick out the top of the elastic of his shorts, he was jerking off in Dr Robert's car on the way across the western plains.

'Careful,' Dr Robert said a little peevishly, aware of both the leather seats of his BMW and the imminent triple-climax that he knew was about to happen.

Too late. With a slightly annoyed frown on his face JD ejaculated — once, twice, three times, up over his front. He then made a little Brazilian moue at the camera phone in his hand, pressed stop and put it down.

'You speak over my cumshot,' he said to Dr Robert, without, it must be admitted, any heat at all.

'Sorry,' Dr Robert said. 'Will you have to do another one?'

JD shrugged, pulled a number of tissues from a box and commenced cleaning up.

JD's cum was astringent and claggy, and Dr Robert could smell it, like some chemical cleaning agent. How virile this young Brazilian was. It made his head go all swimmy just thinking about it.

JD was using a really ridiculous and unnecessary amount of tissues and throwing them off onto the passenger-side floor, Dr Robert noticed, with annoyance. He would have to tell JD to take them out of the car, or else they could conceivably stay there for days.

When he'd done cleaning up JD got busy on his phone — the latest version iPhone, which he was obsessive about keeping fully charged. It was currently connected to the USB port in Dr Robert's car.

'Are you posting it?'

'Editing,' he said, then pouted at the screen, making a face to one side, then the other. 'I might have to do it again. The lighting is no good.'

'What, do it again now?' Dr Robert's ejaculations were few and far between — the idea of two in a row was almost unthinkable.

JD shrugged.

'In a minute.'

'We're stopping in a minute,' Dr Robert said, lifting his chin and indicating the road ahead.

At the mention of their destination, Dr Robert's thoughts went to the zip-lock plastic bag of ashes in the glovebox — the ashes of his sister, Cora — well, a third of the ashes of his sister Cora. The other two thirds were in two zip-lock plastic bags and in the possession of his two remaining sisters, Meredith and Lillian.

He'd forgotten that a third of Cora was in the glovebox, and he blushed.

About ten minutes later, Dr Robert and JD arrived at Mount Elephant. They slowed, put their indicator on and turned in to a gravel driveway with an open gate and a sign beside it in wrought iron that said 'Mount Elephant'. Beyond the gate loomed one of the large humps of mountain that dotted the landscape. They had seen many in the distance during the drive, pimples on the flat and otherwise featureless plains, but this was the first one they had seen close-up. It wasn't large, as mountains go, in fact it was quite moderate, but the fact that it was plonked in the middle of such a vast flatness made it seem incongruous and larger than it was. It was a smooth and featureless mound, slightly flat-topped, without trees, cloaked in the same beige grass as the surrounding paddocks.

'Wow,' said JD, and Dr Robert turned to him. He was apparently genuinely impressed. 'What is this?'

'It's an extinct volcano,' Dr Robert said. 'I told you.'

'Wow. When you say extinct volcano, I didn't think it would be like this.'

What, then, did he think it would be like?

Dr Robert sighed and began to regret bringing JD along on this family excursion to scatter Cora's ashes. Massive dick and a daily triple-cumshot aside, there were limits.

'There's Meredith's car,' said Dr Robert.

*

Meredith, one of Dr Robert's remaining sisters, had decided not to wait for him and JD, and had begun the ascent to the Mount Elephant crater rim on her own. Meredith walked prim and upright, picking her way up the path, careful of her ankles and her patent leather shoes. She wore all black, including a sleeveless dress, a massive hat, which was constantly threatening to blow off, and a pair of Gucci sunglasses so big they looked like two black side-plates on her face. She was a fan of Audrey Hepburn, and had chosen her mourning outfit accordingly. She had her dog, Archie, a French Bulldog, on a long zip-lead, and another third of Cora's ashes in a zip-lock plastic bag in her patent leather handbag.

Meredith was a year and a half older than Dr Robert, but she liked to think she looked about ten years younger. She was thin and acerbic, powdered her face with unbecomingly pale powder, dyed her hair black and wore glasses with brightly coloured frames. (Her Audrey Hepburn sunnies were prescription.) She managed a clothes shop, although she called it a 'flagship store'. She had never been married, had no partner and no children, but did have a great deal of love for her dog.

Meredith was appalled and embarrassed at her brother's continual string of liaisons with what she considered totally inappropriate young men, the last of which was — as she described him in her own head — this 'utterly ridiculous Brazilian creature'.

She had met JD the previous night. She had visited Dr Robert's terrace house in Toorak in order to pick up her third of Cora's ashes before heading out today to Mount Elephant.

Having a gay brother was absolutely fine — in theory. She just wished he would settle down with a man of his own age, some nice, charming, silver fox, George Peppard-y older man, with his own children, perhaps, grown up and left home of course, and with a nice bit of money of his own. Someone she could perhaps be friends with, cook with, travel with, gossip with — connect with. She pictured it all in her head, like a Home Beautiful layout, with herself and her brother's imaginary boyfriend as the central elements in a fabulous spread, styled by her, with Dr Robert on the periphery looking grateful. Instead, there were all these horrible leeching young men, whose charms, though obvious (this latest one seemed to have an obscenely large package) were utterly lost on her. You couldn't connect with them, you couldn't — well, you couldn't take them seriously. Mostly, though, she hated thinking of her brother as being foolish. Robert fell in love with these boys, went all goo-goo eyed about them and then wanted to tell *her* how much he really admired them for one reason or the other, about their troubles and how he was helping them out, usually financially. Her brother, she thought, was a bit of an idiot when it came to men.

She was finding the path up the side of Mount Elephant hard going. It was a track at first, like a dirt road, cut into the side of the mountain. It climbed from the carpark around the incline of the base, then it doubled back upon itself and climbed more steeply up to the top. This part of the path was scrabbly with a strange volcanic gravel, reddish brown and aerated, looking deceptively like some sort of chocolate.

Meredith looked up. She still had a way to go. Oh God this was boring and hot and uncomfortable — and scratching her shoes. She looked back down the mountain to the carpark and saw Dr Robert's BMW pull up — it looked tiny, like a Matchbox car. She wasn't aware she and Archie had walked so far, or come so high. She got out her mobile phone and texted him: 'We've started up to the rim. It's steep! And boring. Lil and Doug are already here. Wave.'

Dr Robert got out of the car, his phone in his hand. After a moment he looked up and waved broadly to Meredith. Meredith waved back with a cheerful little twiddle of her hand.

*

Lillian and Douglas had arrived at Mount Elephant before Meredith and Archie, and long before Dr Robert and JD. They had already traversed the path along the base of the mountain, and climbed up the steep scoria path to the rim. When they first crested the rim they saw what looked like hills all around them, and both of them thought: 'Is this it?' But when they walked a little further the entire crater became visible below them and they realised the hills around them were indeed the rim of the crater, that they were in a sort of dip, or break in the crater.

Lillian caught her breath — she had not realised how big it would be.

Lillian was the oldest of the siblings, then there was the dead sister, Cora, then Meredith, then Robert, the youngest. Lillian had an empty zip-lock bag with traces of human ashes in her backpack next to a thermos of tea and some sandwiches in foil. She had already scattered her third of the ashes at the highest point of the crater rim. It occurred to her as she did so that a third of a human body didn't really amount to all that much ash-wise. It was odd, really, that they'd separated the ashes into three, but apparently that was how Cora's will had been worded, and so that is how it had happened. She had wanted to put the thirds back together in an urn or something, but the other two had suggested they rendezvous here, at Mount Elephant, and scatter their ashes together. But Douglas hadn't wanted to wait about. Douglas had wanted to get it over with.

'So that's that,' Douglas had said in a disagreeable tone, when the ashes had been scattered. 'Are we done?'

If anyone had asked Lillian she'd tell them she loved her husband and that they had enjoyed a happy life, and yet most of the time she was acutely aware that her husband didn't seem to like her much, and was in fact quite irritated with her. He would suddenly yell at her about the way she was eating, or rubbing her hands on her thighs in the car, as if the noise of her hands on her trousers was irritating him. How could the sound of hands rubbing on trousers irritate a person?

It all seemed so odd to her — the anger and irritation inside him. She didn't understand why it was there, but she had learned what might trigger it, and had, mostly, learned to avoid it. When she couldn't avoid it she endured it.

Douglas had never struck her. In fact, he was physically quite protective of her. When they were out he opened doors for her, he shepherded her in restaurants with a hand softly on the middle of her back, he walked on the road side of the footpath when they were out in town. If he had been violent, she told herself, even once, she would have left — but he was never violent, and so she didn't leave. Sometimes she wished he'd hit her, just once, so she would have had a reason to leave. But he hadn't. And they were left, instead, with this to-and-fro of irritated protection and slightly miserable endurance.

Just lately, Lillian was wondering if she was experiencing early onset dementia. She would look at her bookshelf at home — she was a great reader — and she'd know they were her books, that this was her library of books, biographies, classic novels, Victorian horror stories, mystery stories, but she couldn't place a single one of the titles, or the author names, couldn't remember reading a single one of them. The books, her lifetime of reading, all seemed, when she looked at it, just like a weight of paper and card waiting to be pulped. And then something would shift, some shutter would open, she'd see a title and she'd remember the story and she'd find that all the information was there after all.

Or she would walk down the driveway to go to the shop and suddenly not know whether to turn left or right — a walk she'd done through her life countless times. Left? Or right? Both ways seemed unfamiliar, and she found that her entire sense of direction, of her place in the world was gone. Literally, she didn't know where she was. She knew she was in her driveway, but where was that?

It would only last a moment, and then it would all come back and she'd know that, of course, she turned right, then right again to get to the shop for milk.

She had felt like that earlier, when they had first crested the lip of the crater and she had caught her breath. She could see the hollow in front of them, so perfectly rounded, almost like a bowl, or a mortar she had at home that was almost the same colour as the dead grass — it only needed a giant pestle — and she could see the rim of the crater above them, and she knew they were on an extinct volcano, that much was obvious, and she could see a path to the left and a path to the right, each leading up and around the crater in different directions, but just for a moment she didn't know whether they were about to do the walk or had in fact already done the walk.

As she did every other time this happened she stopped dead still and waited for it to pass. It usually passed. Every other time it had passed — waiting in front of her bookshelf, or at the end of her driveway. And this time it did also. They'd just arrived. They were still to do the walk. Douglas, in fact, had turned to the right and was continuing his slow and steady traipse along the path. She followed behind him.

If only he'd hit her, she would have gone.

*

Dr Robert and JD walked the track at the base of the mountain, and then the scoria path up to the lip of the crater relatively quickly. Like a child, JD was excited to be climbing an extinct volcano. He was also very fit, so he fairly tore up the path, stopping to take photos of himself, turning around on the spot to find the best light, the best angle. He did not seem to take pictures of the mountain ahead of them or of the view across the plains behind them.

Dr Robert, while relatively fit himself, was more what he considered fit-for-purpose — he could walk on a flat surface at a brisk pace forever, but give him stairs or a steep incline and he found himself puffing almost instantly. He became red in the cheeks, and struggled to keep up with JD.

At the lip of the crater, JD paused for a second at a sign, and read. Dr Robert, a little way behind him, joined him after a few minutes.

'Is a scoria cone,' JD told him. 'It was formed from a single major volcanic activity somewhere between 5,000 and 20,000 years ago. There would have been a lava lake in the crater, and this where we are standing now, this is where the lava lake breached the cone and flowed out.'

'Very good,' Dr Robert said, catching his breath.

JD went back to his reading. Dr Robert looked up at the rim of the crater above them. His two sisters were both up there, Meredith leading Archie, and Lillian with Doug, but they were not walking together. Meredith and Archie were at the highest point of the lip of the crater up and to his right, and Lil and Doug had continued on around the crater and were now up and to his left. They were so far away they were just little stick figures, silhouettes, but oddly easy to identify even so.

'Damn them,' Dr Robert said. 'Why couldn't they wait for us?'

He was annoyed with Meredith already. She had never been one for the niceties, he knew, and he didn't mind her sharp edges — in fact she could be so wonderfully bitingly funny — but he considered that she had been downright rude to JD last night. She had been dismissive and disdainful. She had looked, all night long, smirky and knowing, as if laughing at him. Sure, her face was slightly odd at the moment and did seem to pull a bit at the sides of the mouth — evidence of new facelift procedures, he deduced — but he knew a smirk when he saw one. At one point, when brother and sister were in the kitchen, and JD left in the other room with the dog, Meredith had said witheringly: 'What *can* you have to talk about?'

It was utterly unfair of her to pass judgement. She was always doing it.

'You see down there?' JD interrupted his thoughts, pointing into the crater. 'The hump at the bottom of the crater, that is the lava plug.'

'Very good,' Dr Robert said without looking. He was madly texting Meredith.

'Wait for us, would you?' he texted.

The dark clad figure up on the peak could be seen to take something out of its pocket and bend towards it for a second or two. Then Dr Robert's phone double-pipped, the sign he had a message.

'Get the Brazilian to piggyback you.'

Oblivious to all this, JD took his shirt off and arranged it around his head like a turban — he had neglected to bring a hat. His exposed torso was magnificent in the nearly noonday sun. His nipples were like chew-toys, his pecs massive. His abs were defined, and there were two bands of muscle disappearing in a V into his low-riding shorts. Dr Robert gazed unabashed at this vision of manhood.

Mine, he thought — but a shadow at the back of that thought knew that JD was nothing of the kind. *Mine for now* might have been more apposite.

The truth of it was, of course, that no, Dr Robert and JD didn't really have much to talk about, but that was hardly the point, was it?

He followed JD off on the right-hand path.

*

Up on the peak of the crater rim, Meredith was reading a small plaque that had been set in concrete, apparently randomly, alongside the path. It was about the size of a shoebox, angled in the ground slightly so that the top was tilted towards the viewer for easy readability. There were the traces of human ashes across the surface, and in the grass around the sides of it. It read:

> *James Jacob Lovejoy of Mount Elephant*
> *27-08-1935 — 4-11-2003*
> *Died here in an accident whilst moving his cattle.*
> *Dearly loved husband of Cora.*

'Cows up here?' she said to herself. 'How awkward.' She tried to imagine cows grazing on the rim of the volcano and failed. How would they get up? She guessed cows could walk up steep hills. She didn't really know much about cows and their physical prowess.

She stepped off the path and closer to the edge of the crater. It looked deceptively gentle, the curved slope down into the bottom, smooth and grassy and soft, like the inner edge of a bowl, but yes, if you fell down there you might get a bit of momentum up, and there were plenty of rocks to hit on the way down. Yes, she thought, very deceptive.

She took the little zip-lock bag of ashes out of her handbag, un-zipped it and, after taking a little moment, tipped her third of Cora's ashes out and over her husband's memorial stone. The breeze immediately began playing with them, swirling them around and off in little driftlets into the air above the crater.

Meredith put a handkerchief to her face, stepped back, turned and looked out and across the plains. She and Archie were right up under the clouds here at the peak — curious, sparsely spaced little flat-bottomed clouds that looked as if they sat on the atmosphere. It felt as if she was closer to the base of the clouds than she was to the land. There was something heady and light about being up this high, under the clouds. She wasn't sure whether it invigorated her or depressed her.

Archie tugged at his lead. He was panting, the poor darling. She took out a bottle of water and a mini dog-dish and gave him a drink. He lapped at it gratefully.

Her mind went back to last night when Dr Robert had a go at Archie. Admittedly Archie had made a bit of a spectacle of himself, humping on JD's leg.

'What breed is it?' Dr Robert had asked with a screwed-up face, as if — ridiculous thought — he was jealous.

'French bulldog,' Meredith had said. 'Off, Archie, bad dog.'

'It's odd, really, how fashions for breeds go,' Dr Robert had said. 'I mean, you never see Afghan Hounds any more, do you?'

'Well, no,' she had agreed, a bit bewildered. 'Archie!'

'Whereas these are a dime a dozen.'

She threw him a withering look.

'If you think about it, it's just like Nazi Germany,' Dr Robert said.

They had laughed at that, and JD had looked at them as if they were mad.

Meredith lifted her sunglasses and peered back to where Dr Robert and JD were on the way up the path to the peak. JD, she noticed, had taken his shirt off and put it on his head as a turban. Even from this distance, seeing them as stick figures, she could sense the sexuality of the man — he oozed it. No wonder Archie had humped his leg — if it was going to be anyone it would be him. And following behind him, a step or two, head down, covered from wrist to neck against the sun, with a slightly-too-large and definitely unfashionable gardening hat on to keep the sun off his pale face, was Robert.

If only he could see himself as she did now, from up under the flat-bottomed clouds, him bent-backed, hunching along in the pheromone-rich wake of a virile, shirtless, eminently hump-able Brazilian. He looked pathetic, even from a distance.

'Come on, Archie,' she said, packing up his bowl. 'Let's keep moving.'

She didn't want to wait for them to catch up.

*

A little further around the rim of the volcano, Douglas had taken his bird glasses out and was staring blatantly across the crater at his sister-in-law, Meredith, and her dog. He'd never liked her much. She wasn't the sort of woman he admired — a jumped up, tarted up, citified kind of woman, with a jumped up citified kind of dog, the sort of dog that really wasn't much use to anybody.

Douglas wasn't a happy man. He had anxiety headaches, a heart murmur, and irritable bowel syndrome. When he and Lillian came out for the day he had to take a pill to seize up his bowel so that he didn't have any trouble. It felt, as a result, as if he was walking around carrying a brick in his abdomen. It was uncomfortable, and made him as irritable as his bowel. His irritability was usually aimed at Lillian. The slightest thing she did annoyed him when he was in this sort of mood. He would begin by feeling a sense of pent-up, formless, shapeless annoyance with her, which would grow into anger, sometimes stifling, and he would then enter into a period of crushing, oppressive silence, until something pushed him over the edge and he snapped at her. It had got so that their waking moments together were a vicious circle of silent treatment, pent up anger, vicious little outbursts over something piddling, and short moments of *détente*. There was no room for tenderness.

The odd thing was that, during those moments of *détente*, he hated himself. He didn't want to hurt her. He really didn't. But he didn't feel able to stop himself. He even had a mantra he chanted in his head when he could feel himself edging into the silent and stony phase. 'Do you want to upset her? No. Then let her go. Do you want to upset her? No. Then let her go.'

But it never seemed to work.

The whole thing was made worse by the fact that they spent almost every moment together ever since he had retired — every waking moment in each other's company, and every sleeping moment lying side by side.

This constant companionship was, surely, he thought, a part of the problem, and yet when she was not around he was utterly lost. A few years ago she had to go into hospital for a number of days to have a mastectomy, and within two days he was in there also, either from a spider bite, or food poisoning, they didn't know. He could barely look after himself. He could not cope without her.

And yet, there it was, every single day there was something about her that caused that formless, shapeless anger to well up inside of him.

The truth was, he was petrified, utterly petrified of what would happen if she died first. He took great comfort in the fact that he was five years older than her and that, anyhow, women generally outlived men in Australia. But still, the thought of her dying first and leaving him to cope obsessed him.

He had known almost all their life together that he loved her more than she loved him. He adored her when she was young, absolutely adored her. She had been so beautiful and spirited. And she had looked at him, not those other fellows, the wealthy landowners and the good-looking townies, not them but him, nothing but a farm labourer. He landed her, he got her, he married her. And they had been happy for a while, for a few years — or more accurately, he had been happy in his cluelessness thinking they were happy. But as soon as he realised that she didn't love him as deeply as he loved her, he couldn't help it, he started to resent her.

When she was out in the garden or cooking or reading a book — she was always reading, and it was one of the things that annoyed him the most — doing anything without him, she looked so serene, so lovely, so happy, so self-sufficient, and he hated it. He began to resent any moment she was alone without him. How had it come to this? All mixed up somehow, all knotted and wrong. He loved her so much, and he treated her so badly. It was horrible. He was horrible.

If only he died first, it would all be okay. And he didn't mind if it came sooner rather than later. He wasn't at all anxious to make old bones.

He turned his bird glasses from Meredith to the other two walkers, who had reached the summit. It was two men, an older man with a floppy hat on and his sleeves rolled down and buttoned at the wrist — must be his brother-in-law, Robert — and a younger lad, some sort of foreigner, with his shirt off and tied about his head. The younger one was gesticulating at the clouds and talking, saying something that came fitfully across the crater to Douglas's ears. He could hear a voice, he could even make out that it was accented, but couldn't make out any words.

'Oh,' he then said, and stopped in his tracks.

Lillian, walking behind him, stopped also.

'What is it?' she asked. Then she too turned and squinted in the direction he was looking. She could see figures on the lip of the crater but couldn't make out anything specific.

'That young chap over there. He's taking his pants off.'

*

Over at the peak JD had indeed taken his pants off. He undid the button and the zip of his shorts, let them drop, then stepped out of them. They were so loose that he didn't have to take his shoes off. He was left wearing only his $915 kicks, his shirt as a turban, and a pair of briefs with a brand name on the band.

Behind him, Dr Robert had only just finished scattering the final third of his sister Cora's ashes from the zip-lock plastic bag. When he turned back he saw JD with his pants off. He stumbled on nothing and held his hands out, palms flat in the international signal to stop whatever the fuck it is that you're doing.

'Stop. Stop that. What are you doing?'

'I think Instagram. The light is good, yes?'

'No. No no no. You can't jerk off up here. I've just scattered my sister's ashes.'

JD wasn't listening. He took a hold of his dick through his underwear and started kneading it, pulling it rhythmically down in his undies like the teat of an udder, working the blood into it. Dr Robert gaped at him, appalled.

'You can't wank up here,' he said.

'No, is for Instagram. Pointing down.'

'Pointing down? It doesn't …'

'I want the fields. I want the — the light — the clouds in the background — I want to be like an angel, you know, floating floating.' He said it *flow-ding*.

'You want what?'

'You be my photographer, yes?' He stepped over and handed Dr Robert his phone. His dick was already massive in his underwear, flolloping from side to side as he walked, and Dr Robert shied away from it like a skittish horse.

JD then dropped to the ground and began rapidly doing push-ups. He had explained this to Dr Robert also. He needed to get a pump up, and get the veins showing in his arms. How long ago it now seemed that these intricacies had been shared and had seemed horny and sweet and harmless.

Dr Robert looked ahead around the crater to where Meredith walked with Archie on his lead. Meredith's back was towards him. She was looking across at the other walkers. Dr Robert followed her gaze and squinted across at Lillian and Douglas. Douglas was looking directly at them through binoculars.

'Get up. Put your clothes on. The others are watching.'

JD jumped up, full of beans, and arranged his underwear, smoothing it over the mound of his dick, making sure the band was straight. He then ran his fingers through his hair, shook his hands out like a gymnast about to run at a pommel horse or something, and struck a pose.

Dr Robert forgot his agitation for a second.

'Oh God,' he breathed.

He had to admit, the guy knew how to strike a pose. His shoulders were rounded, hunched, and he was obviously clenching each and every muscle that he could clench, his pecs, his abs, the muscles all along his arms, every muscle shown to perfect advantage, and yet he contrived to look as though he was just mooching around, standing with one hand on his hip, his head turned slightly to one side, gazing off into the distance — *flow-ding, flow-ding* on the clouds. It looked good.

'Oh fuck it,' Dr Robert said, and he flung off his too big, too floppy gardening hat with abandon. He took JD's phone and crouched down low to the ground, so that he could get a picture looking up at JD, so that the clouds would indeed be in the background, and everything else, the muscles, the bulge, would be shown to best advantage. Dr Robert took a couple of photos.

'Step back a bit,' he said.

Which is when the inevitable happened. JD stepped back, knocked one heel into the shoebox shaped plaque set in the ground as a memorial to Cora Lovejoy's husband, and fell over backwards into the crater. Dr Robert was left taking a picture of bare sky with flat-bottomed clouds.

'Hang about,' Douglas said, over the other side of the crater, still looking through his binoculars. 'He's pitched over.'

Meredith, at this point, seeing Douglas looking intently at something behind her, turned and saw JD backwards-somersaulting down into the crater.

'Shit,' she said.

Dr Robert made off over the edge and tried to walk down at a safe pace, putting his hand down and back to steady himself against the earth, but the slope and his momentum made him unable to stop himself breaking into a rough shamble.

'Don't run!' Meredith shouted urgently. She had a loud voice and Dr Robert heard her, but he ignored her and continued shambling and eventually galloping down the incline.

'Oh, the idiot,' she said more quietly to Archie, who had come up beside her. 'He'll be arse over tit himself next.'

She got her phone out and called 000.

Around the other side of the rim of the crater Lillian was squinting.

'Is that …' Lillian began. 'That's not Robert, is it?'

'No, it's his friend. Another of his little foreign chaps.'

They were just at the point in the path where it began to descend towards the break in the crater. From there it was an easy couple of minutes down to the base of the crater bowl. Lillian made off at a cracking pace and Douglas, making heavy work of it, followed.

At the bottom of the crater, JD lay prone and naked except for his $915 crocodile-embossed low-rise sneakers. His shirt, which had been around his head as a turban had come off on the way down. His underwear, which must have torn down one side when his hip hit a rock, was around one knee, bloodied and half shredded. There were bloody scratches all over his body, and a couple of deeper, more concerning looking wounds. One leg — Dr Robert gave an involuntary moan when he saw it — was at an odd angle and looked to have been broken at the shin. There was the white of bone amongst the blood. JD's cock was lying across his hip, unharmed. Flaccid, it was sweet and silky and soft, and Dr Robert thought it made him seem terribly vulnerable.

Dr Robert shook himself out of his funk. He knelt down beside JD, slapped his face and called his name. He felt for a pulse at his neck and for breath against his own cheek. JD moaned and moved his head to the side, but then lay still again.

Lillian was just arriving.

'He's alive,' Dr Robert said.

'Thank goodness,' Lillian breathed.

Meredith arrived a moment later, brandishing her phone.

'I've called emergency and they're on the way,' she said. 'I can't get any signal down here, so I'll have to go back up. Call cut out on the way down. What's the situation?' She was focused and in control. In fact, she was totally in her element.

'He's responding,' Dr Robert said. 'He's cut up a bit, but doesn't seem to be losing too much blood. Broken tibia.'

'They said not to move him,' Meredith said, and moved to head back up by the shortest route. After a second she turned back. 'They're sending a helicopter.'

'What?' Dr Robert said.

'They're airlifting him out. Have to, apparently. It's happened before and it's too hard over land. They had schoolkids here a while back and the same thing happened.'

Meredith turned back and began her slow ascent up the side of the crater, shouting for Archie, who had taken the opportunity to make a break for it and rush about dangerously, trailing his lead behind him.

There was a moment or two of complete silence after Meredith started up the path. Lilian and Dr Robert both noticed it — there was no sound down here. No crickets in the ground, no birdsong, not even the sound of the wind. Just silence and stillness and a feeling that nothing living bothered to venture down here. They looked up at the rim of the crater above them. From down here it looked so much deeper than it did from up above. Deep and encircled by the earth, close and oppressive, with only a few of those weird flat-bottomed clouds directly above them, like a lid on a jar.

A puffing sound interrupted the silence. It was Douglas, finally joining them.

'Saw it happen. Just tripped,' he panted.

Neither of them answered him, but Lillian took off her neckerchief, unfurled it, flapped it once in the still air, then moved forward and laid it gently over JD's exposed dick.

Douglas, red in the face, with one hand at his chest, made a little groan of surprise, then had a massive heart attack and pitched over dead.

*

Park Rangers came over land, and the emergency services came by air. Both bodies were strapped into gurneys and lifted one after the other. It took only minutes once they arrived, and soon after that the helicopter pitched slightly and took off in the direction of Geelong Base Hospital. There was no room for any of the able-bodied parties in the helicopter, so they would soon have to make their way to the hospital over land — a question of an hour drive back the way they had come.

The three remaining siblings, Lillian, Meredith and Dr Robert, left standing in the bottom of the crater, were bereft. Dr Robert was exhausted, having performed CPR on Douglas to no avail. The happenings of the afternoon had been outlandish and slightly surreal — none of them could quite grasp it.

The three of them were not close. They rarely saw each other. When they did it was prickly and difficult, and each felt that the others misunderstood them, or, worse still, disapproved, and yet in this moment they were completely united. They even looked more similar than they ever had — refined and slender, pale, almost white-grey, and blank-faced. They found they were holding hands, all three of them, something they had never ever before done.

In the back of Lillian's mind, behind her shock, was a sense of utter hopelessness. With the death of her husband, she had lost all stability, all certainty. She felt just like she did at the end of her driveway when one of those spells overtook her — she had no concept of her place in the world, her spot on the earth, which way to turn, left or right. She had always wanted to leave Douglas, dreamed of leaving, but she knew that now Douglas was gone she was lost and she would never know herself again.

In the back of Dr Robert's mind was a kernel of clarity, one that he had been granted thanks to the accident, in which he saw himself as he was, saw JD for what he was, and understood their relationship fully. He knew that, when he was mended, JD could, if he wanted to, make a permanent home with him at the terrace in Toorak.

Meredith, holding a severely reprimanded Archie under her arm, was thinking of their dead sister, Cora, and of how the wind had swirled her ashes, blown them into the air, and that, presumably, they had settled down here, at the bottom of the crater.

QWERTY

I had been working as a transcriber for about five years at ATS, Australiawide Transcribing Services (yes, they do write Australiawide as one word), when I picked up a fifteen minute audio file from the queue, started typing and became — well, there's really only one way to say it — obsessed. The case in question was *Hsu vs Cronshaw*, which you may remember from the news around the middle of last year. It was a charge of statutory rape brought by the defendant, Mr Andrew (Andy) Hsu, intern at Steggle & Allen Legal, one of the largest legal firms in Melbourne, against Mr Lewis Cronshaw, one of many junior partners in the firm.

I transcribe across many jurisdictions and courts. Coroner's Court, Magistrate's Court, Family Court, Children's Court, and County Court.

Coroner's Court is probably my favourite. That sounds a bit morbid, and I guess it is, but it's just like reading a murder mystery or watching *CSI* or something — death one step removed. I think I'm immune to it. Typing a Coroner's Court case makes me realise that there are so many more ways of dying than any of us could possibly imagine.

A close second favourite is the VROs, the violence restraining orders, in the Magistrate's Court. Some of the time they're very tragic, especially when it's about domestic violence — those women, because it's usually women, I feel very sad for. But some of the time, when it's just about a fight over a fence, or a punch-up at a party, they're hilarious. It's like my own reality TV show, the VROs, sort of trash-television. The ridiculous bickerings that go on between neighbours or family members, or fights that are happening between this white trash piece of shit and that white trash piece of shit — both with full recourse to the law. It's funny. And then tragic. And then funny again. Just like reality TV.

Family Court is the only one I really dislike. Not all the time, but most of the time it's just disagreeable people who can't get on and won't cut each other even the smallest bit of slack.

The audio we all want to pick up, though, is County Court. That's where all the juiciest criminal cases are tried, the ones that are in all the papers. If you're really lucky, you get assigned to a daily, which is where we type and merge and deliver the court transcripts same day. So the audio comes in straight from the court room, it's allocated in fifteen minute chunks to only a few typists — it's considered better to have fewer typists on the dailies so they become familiar with the case and the witnesses and the prosecutor and defence and the whole thing — and you sit there all day and just immerse yourself in the case, the one that'll be in tomorrow's headlines. Sure, you never get to hear the whole lot, because other typists are working on the case at the same time as you, but if you're working on it all day, you get maybe five or six fifteen minute blocks, and you get the gist.

The audio we get from the County Court comes with video — it's really basic video, like it's been filmed on CCTV, but it's video. It's meant to help us get the audio down, if we can see the lips of the witnesses actually moving, I suppose. But it also makes it feel even more like reality TV, which is why I like County the best.

The *Hsu vs Cronshaw* trial was a case in the County Court, it was a daily, and I was assigned to it. All the ATS stars were aligning for me that day.

*

At ATS, when you get in you clock on — you literally clock on. Not like they used to do in a factory, by punching a card into a machine, but by logging on to your computer. When you log in, it's recorded centrally, and they know you're at work and ready to be assigned audio. Then you put your earphones on and you get your audio, you set up your file and you just type. It takes me about an hour to type 15 minutes of audio, which isn't great, but isn't bad either.

There are about twenty of us on the floor at ATS in Melbourne, and I have to say, we're a motley bunch. I don't know what it is, but as a job this tends to attract the waifs and the strays of the world, of which I am undoubtedly one. Knowledge of the law does actually help now and then, I admit, and of course you have to type super-fast and have a good ear, but apart from that, you don't have to be very skilled — with apologies to my co-workers. Also, you don't have to look at another person all day, let alone talk to anyone. In other words the job is perfect for the socially maladjusted, like me.

Until ATS, I hadn't been able to hold down a job for any length of time. I'm incredibly awkward, but alongside this I have a weird tell-it-like-it-is kind of blunt honesty thing going on. This means I'm either unsure of what to say and say nothing, or, if I do say something, I often say the wrong thing, usually something offensive or offhand. I can't really judge people, or judge what's appropriate with people — I can't read a room — and it can make for some really horrible moments in the workplace. I also tend to obsess about things, deadlines, other people and whether they like me or not, my inability to speak easily to people, things like that, and this has in the past spiralled into severe anxiety, and from there it's only a short tram-ride to depression. So yeah, not exactly super-employable.

I had a late-in-life diagnosis of Asperger's and that's when it all began to make sense. I'm on the spectrum — I know you probably roll your eyes a bit at that one, and yes, it is a term that is bandied around a bit too freely, and yes, we are all on the spectrum somewhere — but I really value my diagnosis, in a way, because it helped make sense of what I was beginning to think of as a whole slew of personality flaws. It's not a flaw, it's just Asperger's. I'm no different now than before my diagnosis, but I understand myself a bit better and that's been a real relief, I have to say.

ATS suits me, the circumstances of the work suit me. I feel like a misfit amongst misfits, none of whom I have to talk to. It's perfect.

A quick bit about me. I'm just about to turn 30, I live in a studio apartment in Melbourne's North. I have no savings and own no property apart from a bed that can be lifted up into the wall, which I love and have wanted since I was a kid. I have a massive collection of movie memorabilia and spend a lot of time online. I have zero friends. I mean, I have acquaintances and people I speak to, but they are either in the medical profession, or my mother, or the cleaning lady my mother sends to my house, or, well, maybe the guy who serves me coffee every morning at Espress-n-go in town near work. I guess there is Allison at work. She says good morning, I say good morning, and that's about it. She smiles a lot. She seems nice, actually, and normal, and as if she'd like to have a sandwich with me in the park, but I manage to avoid her. I'm not sure what's wrong with her — there must be something, otherwise she wouldn't be at ATS with the rest of us misfits.

I am Chinese-Australian, second generation. My mum and dad have broken up, but I'm still in touch with my mum. In fact, she's around quite a lot, checking that I'm showering and flossing and, well, basically still alive. I have no other family here in Australia.

I have a little Chi Pom cross called Ollie. He's officially a support dog, and I got him to take around with me to keep me calm, but I stopped doing it, I'm afraid to say, because it wasn't working out. I got so much attention on the train and at work, with people always coming up and asking his name and if they could pat him, and stuff, that he was sort of being counter-productive and causing me extra stress instead of calming me down. So yeah, Ollie stays at home all the time now, unless it's a real emergency. He doesn't seem to mind, though. When I leave the house in the morning, I leave him on his bed, and I get the impression he powers down like a droid or something, until he hears my keys in the door and powers back up again. There's never any food eaten or poos taken while I'm out. I wish I could power down like a droid. It would save a lot of worry.

*

The first day of the *Hsu vs Cronshaw* case started just like every other day at ATS. I got the train in to town, walked a few blocks, got a long black from Espress-n-go. I then went upstairs, said a glancing side-swipe of a 'hi' to Allison on the way to the tearoom to fill up my ATS water bottle from the chilled tap, then went back to my seat and logged on.

I saw only one job in my in-box, CRONSHd. It was a daily and it had just started. A couple of other typists had already taken audio, so I went in and took 15 minutes. I could have taken a longer chunk, but I didn't want to do that until I saw what type of case it was. If it was boring or too difficult, I'd just take smaller chunks and try and leave it for others to take until it was over. I only take a big chunk of audio if it's easy and interesting and will keep my word count up.

I put my noise-cancelling headphones on, opened a new document, and set it up with all the right macros for the names and titles for those appearing. It was before Judge Daisy Macindoe who would be in my transcript as HER HONOUR. She was good for a laugh sometimes. For the defendant was BUCHANAN, MS, who spoke quickly but quite audibly, and was good for word count if you could keep up. For the accused was O'CONNOR, MR, who was a right arsehole and who paused too much to be really good for word count. So far it could go any which way.

I got my foot peddle in the right spot, relaxed my shoulders, let my eyes drift off out the window into the street below — I ignored the video for the most part during the preliminaries — poised my fingers over the keyboard, pressed the pedal and started typing.

The first fifteen minutes went fast. It was good audio and I'd got in early enough to get some nice quick stuff up the front of the case, where the judge was taking appearances and addressing the jury.

I submitted my first turn — that's what we call the audio we take, the document we type — and took some more audio. I saw from the log that we were into evidence of the complainant, Andy Hsu, and so I took a big chunk, 20 minutes, because evidence is good for word count, re-adjusted my headphones and started in.

As I said before, audio from County Court comes with video. We see the top of the witness box, with various microphone stands on it, usually a plastic cup of water for the witness to drink, and a background of wood panelling. The witness is harshly lit from directly above, so their face appears almost white-lit, with the features standing out as if painted on. It's quite harsh and unforgiving, and it makes the whole thing look like an interrogation.

As soon as I saw Andy come onto the witness stand, with the court staff still adjusting the microphones around him, bonking them on the edge of the stand and trying to work out which cord went with what, I knew he was going to be a sad-case and a bad witness.

'Poor Andy.' That's the first thing I thought. 'You don't have a hope.'

He was Chinese-Australian, I'd say, just like me, with black hair and an angular jaw. When he eventually sat down he looked like a deer in the headlights, blank-faced and wide-eyed. He fidgeted, looked at the light, squinted, looked from left to right, and eventually settled down. He seemed like a boy, slight and angular, slumped forward in his chair. I imagined his hands, although I couldn't see them, were thrust between his knees and clamped tight. He had that sort of look about him.

When Miss Buchanan started in with the questioning, she did so gently and with much repetition — obviously a strategy to put Andy at his ease. It seemed to work, and his answers began to come much more readily, although throughout he seemed almost crushingly embarrassed about what he was doing. I sympathised. I'd be a basket case myself if I ever had to take the stand.

Andy's evidence came out very clearly. He told the story of what had happened on the night in question. It was a Friday and after work he had been out with friends to a movie. Did they go out after the movie at all? No. For dinner? No, they had stuff to eat at the movie. It was Gold Class. They had wedges and hot dogs and Sprite. (Like teenagers, I thought, typing.) And what did they do after the movie? Nothing. They all went home. They walked one friend to her apartment building, then Andy and another male friend went to a train station where they parted company and went home on different trains.

BUCHANAN, MS: What time was this? - - - Around 11.

(That's how we type a court transcript, by the way — surname, salutation, colon, question, question mark and three dashes, answer. You'll get used to it.)

And had you been drinking at all — I mean alcohol, not Sprite? - - - No. I don't drink.

You mean you don't drink alcohol? - - - No.

And you didn't drink any that night? - - - No.

And what time did you get home? - - - Around 11.30.

Quite an early Friday night for a 21 year old? - - - I don't — I don't go out much.

We type the words, just the words. And the video, it shows very little. None of it captures the tone. However, it was in that pause, which I typed simply as a dash, where all the emotion was: *I don't — I don't go out much.* A little catch in his voice, a little throb, a moment where he gave himself away. It was in that moment, that dash, that I interpreted a whole lot that was unsaid. Somehow that pause, that throb, told me that Andy was a lot like me, apart from just being Chinese-Australian. He didn't drink, he didn't go out much, he was obviously a quiet, nervy type — and yet he found himself here, in court, in the witness box. It was, that catch in his voice said, almost overwhelming for him.

Miss Buchanan moved quickly on. I could hear, somehow, that something had shifted and the court was — well, I wouldn't say it was on Andy's side, but there was certainly a lot more awareness in the court that Andy was very overwhelmed, very upset, and possibly close to not coping. Judge Macindoe asked Andy if he would like a moment to compose himself. When he said no, she asked Miss Buchanan to move on, please.

Miss Buchanan asked questions of Andy about himself, his background, his study, and how he came to work at Steggle & Allan. He had studied law, he said, and was taken on as an intern at Steggle & Allan just a year ago. When she first asked about the accused, Miss Buchanan was very gentle.

BUCHANAN, MS: And what was your working relationship with Mr Cronshaw? - - - He was my boss.

Your boss. And what — perhaps the best way to ask it is how much did you have to do with Mr Cronshaw on a day to day basis? - - - I don't …

HER HONOUR: Perhaps you can re-phrase the question.

BUCHANAN, MS: Did you see Mr Cronshaw, in the office, every day? - - - Most days.

Did you speak to Mr Cronshaw, in the office this is, every day? - - - Yes — well, perhaps not every day. Sometimes I would get on with my work, or take work from someone else, or — sometimes he was away. Not there.

I see. And what can you tell us about — I'm sorry, I'll rephrase that — were there any moments where — were there any times where you felt uncomfortable with anything Mr Cronshaw said or did to you or in your hearing?

Ms Buchanan was rephrasing on the run, trying hard not to put a question in such a way that there could be an objection made. She was obviously trying not to lead the witness, and yet needed to give him an opening to speak about something.

HER HONOUR: I'm not sure that's very clear, Miss Buchanan. Can you take it one at a time, perhaps?

BUCHANAN, MS: Did Mr Cronshaw ever say anything to you that made you feel uncomfortable — in the office this is? - - - Yes.

Can you tell us please, in your own words, what was said? - - - He said that he'd like to get me over a barrel.

He said he'd like to get you over a barrel? - - - Yes.

What was the context of this comment? - - - We'd been talking about a client, there were a few of us, and someone said that someone else, this client, had them — us I mean, Steggle & Allan, over a barrel. That's when he looked at me and he smirked and I knew he meant …

O'CONNOR, MR: Objection, your Honour.

HER HONOUR: Sustained. Miss Buchanan, we can't …

BUCHANAN, MS: Yes, your Honour. I understand. Yes. If I could go on?

HER HONOUR: Please.

BUCHANAN, MS: Mr Hsu, if you could tell us, please, only what was said. Only the words that were said? - - - Well, he didn't …

What did he say to you? - - - Well, he didn't say anything, but he looked at me as if …

O'CONNOR, MR: Objection, your Honour.

HER HONOUR: Sustained. Miss Buchanan, we might have to move on from this point.

That's what it's like sometimes in these cases. Witnesses are so keen to tell what they interpreted, what they 'know' rather than what they've seen or heard. And it's not evidence so it can't be admitted.

Miss Buchanan moved Andy on, and I could see that he was slightly frustrated by not being able to explain to the court what had happened. She got around it in the end, by getting Andy to describe how he felt — embarrassed, ashamed — without entering into evidence that a look had in fact happened at all. Not, I thought, a very telling point, but all she could do with it at that stage.

She moved on to her second point.

BUCHANAN, MS: And were there any times when anything was done to you, and I mean physically, by Mr Cronshaw, in the workplace, that made you feel intimidated or uncomfortable? - - - Yes, there was. Quite a lot.

Can you describe these things to me? - - - Well, he would often come past me when I was — well, in the copy room or the compactus, which is a filing system — I'm not sure if you know.

I think we're all familiar? - - - And he would move up close to me and reach up past me to a shelf or a file that he pretended to need …

O'CONNOR, MR: Objection, your Honour.

BUCHANAN, MS: Andy, only what was said or done, please. He would reach up past you and what would he do then? - - - He'd say something like …

O'CONNOR, MR: Objection, your Honour.

BUCHANAN, MS: Andy, if you could tell us what he said. Not 'something like'. Think of one time. Let's take the compactus time. What did he say or do that time? - - - It happened a number of times in the compactus.

It was interminable. I was speeding along, typing like a maniac, smoke coming off my keyboard, but it was so frustrating to listen to. The court, I could hear, was getting frustrated as well. Miss Buchanan's tone had become even more flat and careful than it had been earlier. Mr O'Connor continued objecting whenever he could, and his voice was like a computer or something, no emotion — just: *Objection, your Honour.* And Andy, he just couldn't get the hang of it. He kept talking in generalisations or saying what he thought Cronshaw meant, none of which was able to be admitted in evidence.

Bit by bit, slowly, Miss Buchanan drew the evidence out. On one occasion, about a week or so before the offence that Cronshaw was alleged to have committed, Cronshaw had come into the compactus alongside Andy, had come up very close to him, had reached up for a file above him, and in doing so came into contact with him — touched him.

BUCHANAN, MS: Where did he touch you? - - - He touched me on the — he touched me on the back — the back of my — he touched me on my bum.

Your bum. What part of him touched your bum, do you know? - - - His hand.

You definitely felt his hand? - - - Yes. His hand.

And was his hand — I'm sorry Andy, but it's necessary to get this clear — what part of his hand touched you on the bum? - - - It was his — it was his thumb.

His thumb? - - - Yes.

And what part of your bum did he touch with his thumb? - - -

It was at this precise moment that my audio ran out. I couldn't believe it. Talk about cliff-hanger. I looked at the time — I'd been typing flat out for an hour. I looked at my word count and it was well above my usual hourly target. I had about ten or fifteen minutes before I had to get typing again, so I kept listening to the audio file, watching the little square of video.

It came out at length that no, Cronshaw didn't simply pat Andy on the bum-cheek or anything like that, no, he jabbed his thumb right up against Andy's bumhole. Andy gave his evidence blank-faced. He was either stoic or stunned — it was hard to tell in the video we had — so over-lit and harsh, the contrast too high. His eyes were black and inscrutable, his lips were large and quite pink. There was no discernible emotion on that face.

*

I had to get typing again. I went in and took another chunk of audio. Other typists had taken sections directly after what I'd just typed, but I grabbed another twenty minutes from later in the file — it was still Miss Buchanan taking the evidence of Andy Hsu. It looked like it might be Andy all day at this rate — we hadn't even got to Mr O'Connor and cross-examination, yet.

I got myself all sorted out, pressed the pedal and started typing. Andy was now giving evidence about later in the night, after he had got home from the movies. The first words I typed were:

O'CONNOR, MR: Objection, your Honour.

So I back-pedalled a bit to hear what had come before. Given how quick I was typing, I knew I could catch up word count later. It turned out that when he had got home from the movies Andy had watched Netflix for a while, half watching, half doodling around on his laptop, posting a review of the movie they had seen earlier in the night. And then he had gone to bed. He was unclear about what time it was, and though he said he could guess, he was not allowed to do so. All that could be said in evidence was that it was around midnight or some time thereafter.

He then said he was awoken by a knock on his door. Again, he said he didn't know what time it was, but that he had definitely been deeply asleep and that the knock had woken him up with a jolt. He didn't know who it could be, and was not expecting anyone, but he went to the door and opened it. He didn't have a peep hole in his door, which led directly out to a balcony with steps down to the street. It was a shared balcony running along the building with two other flats opening up onto that balcony.

When Andy opened the door, it was Lewis Cronshaw and he was drunk, according to Andy. And that's when O'Connor had objected. I took up the typing from there.

BUCHANAN, MS: What did you observe? How was Mr Cronshaw acting? - - - He was wobbly on his feet and slurring his words. I could also smell alcohol on his breath.

It seemed that Andy had become accustomed to O'Connor's objections and to the right way to give evidence between the last bit of audio I typed and this. Miss Buchanan went on with her questions, and it came out that Cronshaw had insisted he be let in. Andy had let him in, even though the whole thing made him feel awkward and a little bit intimidated, because he didn't want to wake his neighbours or cause a scene. Once inside, Cronshaw had approached Andy and tried to kiss him.

BUCHANAN, MS: And what did you say? - - - I said no, and moved away.

You said 'no'? - - - I said no.

You very definitely said the word 'no'? - - - I did, yes.

After that, it was Andy's evidence that Cronshaw moved away. He apologised, he asked Andy's forgiveness for busting in on him like that. He was very sorry, he said. He was drunk, he said.

BUCHANAN, MS: Any objections, Mr O'Connor?

O'CONNOR, MR: Not at this time, no.

HER HONOUR: Carry on, Miss Buchanan. And please don't speak directly to counsel.

BUCHANAN, MS: And what did you say to him then? - - - I said it was okay, but that he should go.

You said it was okay? - - - Yes.

What did you mean by that? - - - I meant I accepted his apology.

And that he should go? - - - Yes.

And what did he say to that? - - - He asked if he could use the toilet.

And what did you say? - - - I said yes.

And what did he do? - - - He went to the toilet.

I noticed a change in tone here, as if everything started going in super-slow-motion. We were obviously approaching a critical point. The court heard that Cronshaw went to the toilet. We heard that Hsu stayed in the lounge-room. We heard that Cronshaw flushed and came back to the lounge-room. We heard that Hsu moved towards the door to open it for him. We heard that Cronshaw came up behind him and pinned Hsu's arms to his side, turned him around and began kissing him again. We heard that Hsu wriggled, struggled, tried to free himself from Cronshaw's grip. We heard that Cronshaw forced him, still holding his arms pinioned, to the bedroom, and there pushed him onto the bed and forced him to have sex. The mechanics of the sex was gone into at some length, and during those questions and answers, Andy Hsu was stony-faced but cooperative and clear.

BUCHANAN, MS: And did you say 'no' at any point after the time when he had first tried to kiss you? - - - I don't think so.

Can you tell the court why you didn't say 'no' again? - - - I was stunned.

You were stunned? Anything else? - - - I was intimidated. I felt as if I was going to get in trouble. Or hurt or something.

You thought that Mr Cronshaw might hurt you if you said 'no'? - - - Well, I thought he might, yes. Yes, I did.

Did you say anything at all to him? Anything? - - - Yes, I did.

What did you say? - - - I said 'You shouldn't do this. You'll regret it.'

And when did you say that to him? - - - When he was — when I was under him in the bed.

And did he say anything to you? - - - No, he didn't speak at all.

And that's when my second lot of audio finished.

*

The last part of Andy Hsu's evidence I typed that day was cross-examination by Mr O'Connor. I wasn't sure how this was going to go. Andy was doing okay with his own counsel who led him gently by the hand, but when the gloves were off, I was not sure how he'd cope.

Mr O'Connor passed over all of the workplace incidents completely. Instead, he began a line of questioning on a topic that had not so far been covered. It appeared to take Andy completely off-guard.

O'CONNOR, MR: Did you ever socialise with Mr Cronshaw after work? - - - Socialise?

Yes? - - - I'm not sure what you mean.

Surely you understand, Mr Hsu, what socialise means. Did you ever do anything at all with Mr Cronshaw outside of work? - - - Like what?

That's for you to say, Mr Hsu. If you could just answer the question, please. Did you ever socialise with Mr Cronshaw outside work? - - - Well, not specifically, no. I mean, I never — not just me and him, no.

Not just the two of you? - - - No.

But perhaps in a group? Did you socialise with him in a group outside of work? - - - Yes, in a group setting, yes I did.

So you did socialise with Mr Cronshaw outside of work. And what did you do in this group setting outside of work with Mr Cronshaw? - - - Well, after work on a Friday sometimes, a few of us would go out to a bar. Around the corner from work.

To a bar. A few of you? - - - Yes, a few of us.

You don't drink? - - - No, I don't drink.

But you went to a bar? - - - Yes. I drank soft.

All the time? - - - Well, once or twice, I had — if it was someone's birthday or something and a round of drinks were bought, then sometimes I would have one — so as not to be rude. Just have a sip or two and leave it.

So when you told this court that you don't drink alcohol, that wasn't, in fact, true, was it Mr Hsu?

HER HONOUR: Does anything turn on this, Mr O'Connor? If not, then I'd like you to move on, please. I'm satisfied with Mr Hsu's explanation about after work drinks, and looking forward to my own gin and tonic, actually, so if we could please get on?

O'CONNOR, MR: Certainly, your Honour. And did you speak with Mr Cronshaw on these occasions, out at after work drinks on a Friday? - - - Well, I'm not sure — what do you mean?

I mean, Mr Hsu, did you speak with Mr Cronshaw on these after work drinks occasions — it's not a difficult question? - - - Yes, I suppose I did.

Suppose? - - - I did, then. Yes, I did. Of course. I did speak to him. I don't see what …

HER HONOUR: If you could just answer the questions as put to you, please, Mr Hsu, as accurately as possible.

It went on a bit in this way for some time. Mr O'Connor skated dextrously close to the wind on a few occasions, and Miss Buchanan got a few of her own objections in, but the upshot of it all was that Cronshaw and Hsu quite regularly went out after work on a Friday, in a group, and quite regularly spoke tete-a-tete together. It was like pulling teeth to get Hsu to admit to it, but eventually he did. However, it was impossible to get much out of Andy about what they'd spoken about. Just stuff, nothing much, nothing special, work and what they were doing that weekend.

O'Connor skipped on then and went right to Cronshaw's visit to Hsu's flat and the kissing that had happened almost immediately after Hsu had opened the door.

O'CONNOR, MR: So you said 'no', when Mr Cronshaw took you in his arms and kissed you? - - - Yes.

How did you say it? - - - I don't know, I just said it.

What precise words did you say? - - - I said, 'No,' just the one word, and moved away.

And did you say it firmly? - - - Firmly?

Yes, did you say it loudly and firmly? - - - Well, I don't know. I don't think I did.

Did you say it quietly? - - - Yes, I suppose I said it more quietly. I didn't want to be rude. I didn't want to embarrass him.

You didn't want to embarrass him? - - - No.

So you said it quietly. He's kissing you, and you said it quietly. Did you say it, perhaps, teasingly? - - - I beg your pardon?

Teasingly — as a bit of sexy teasing? Did you say it in that way? - - - No, I just said it in a normal way. I said no. I didn't shout it because it was very late at night and I was embarrassed and I didn't want to disturb the neighbours, but I said it. I said no, and that should have been enough.

Andy brought his hand up and passed it over his eyes. I wasn't sure from watching the video if he was crying, or whether he was just trying to calm himself. The judge asked him again if he wanted a break, and again he said no, he didn't.

I thought it odd that Mr O'Connor was pressing this point, I must admit, because it was the one time that Andy was absolutely certain he had said 'no', the one time, in fact, that he had been crystal clear about denying consent. Giving him a second chance to express this to the court, and in what had turned out to be so firm a manner, so emotional a manner, it seemed like a mistake, a miss-step. But O'Connor was crafty, as became immediately obvious.

O'CONNOR, MR: And after Mr Cronshaw had taken you in his arms and kissed you — an unwelcome advance, you say — after he'd done this and after you had said 'no', quietly, what did he do? - - - What did he do?

Yes, what did he do? - - - Well, he stopped.

So you said no and he stopped — is that right? - - - Well, yes, that time, but later …

I'm just wanting to get the sequence of events clear for the court — you said no to the kissing, and he stopped, is that correct? - - - Yes. That's correct.

Mr O'Connor, having made his point, moved on quickly. Get in, make your point, get out. It was his modus operandi. He skipped ahead, admitting in passing that the sexual act had in fact occurred, to the only other words that Andy Hsu had admitted to speaking, and again shone the spotlight on those.

O'CONNOR, MR: According to your own evidence earlier today, the only other words spoken by you were, 'You should go' and then later, actually during the sexual act, 'You shouldn't do this. You'll regret it.' Would you agree that these words are not the same as 'no'? - - Well, the intention was 'no'.

'Should go.' 'Shouldn't do this.' Neither of those is the same as 'no' is it? - - - What I meant by that was ...

Should and shouldn't implies a choice to be made, doesn't it? - - - No, it doesn't.

HER HONOUR: I'm going to stop you there, Mr O'Connor.

Judge Macindoe quite rightly said that Mr Hsu had made himself clear to the court and should not be asked the same question again. Unfortunately, Mr O'Connor had also made himself clear to the court. He may have been splitting hairs, but it did raise the question of whether Andy Hsu had in fact denied consent.

But Mr O'Connor saved the best for last. He made another rapid left-hand-turn.

O'CONNOR, MR: Can you tell the court, Mr Hsu, how Mr Cronshaw knew where you lived?

Andy opened his mouth but said nothing. He looked off the edge of the little square of video on my screen in the direction of the judge.

HER HONOUR: Just answer the questions as best you can, Mr Hsu.

O'CONNOR, MR: Can you tell the court, Mr Hsu, how Mr Cronshaw knew where you lived? Had he been there before? - - - It was a group thing. A group of us …

Had he been there before? Just a yes or no might get us going in the right direction if you could? - - - Yes he had. He had been there before.

With a group you say? - - - Yes, that's right. From work. After drinks one night a few of us came back to my flat.

Yes, kicking on — is that right? - - - Well, no. Not kicking on. A group of us, we live over this side of town — I mean my side of town — and we shared a taxi. In the taxi we decided we were hungry and I ordered takeaway to be delivered to my place.

Takeaway? - - - That's right. Thai.

And when you say a group, how many of you were there? - - - There were three of us.

So you, Mr Cronshaw and one other person? - - - Yes.

And did that other person also have takeaway Thai with you? - - - No, she — she had to get home. She kept the taxi and went straight on.

So in fact it wasn't a group thing, it was you and Mr Cronshaw only, is that right? - - - Yes, it is.

And how long did he stay? - - - Not long. Hardly any time.

You're sure he didn't stay the night? - - - No. No he didn't.

Did he try to kiss you on that occasion? - - - Yes, actually. Yes, he did. After we'd finished eating he — he tried.

And what did you say? - - - I said 'no' and he stopped.

Andy was getting agitated in the witness box. He was wriggling in his seat.

You are quite sure you said the word 'no'? - - - I'm not — I can't really remember. I may have said something else.

Did you in fact say the words 'we shouldn't'? - - - I don't — I might have said something like that, actually, yes. On that occasion.

Might have said something like that or did in fact say that? - - - Yes. Actually — yes, I said that.

Said 'we shouldn't'? - - - Yes.

Nothing further, your Honour.

And Mr O'Connor was out.

*

There was no more audio to type that day on the *Hsu vs Cronshaw* trial. The judge wrapped early, but instructed the court to reconvene a little earlier the next day to get the next witness done in plenty of time. It was to be Lewis Cronshaw's turn to give evidence.

Myself and the various other typists assigned had finished off the job in plenty of time, typing the audio up almost as soon as it drip-fed through, so that it could be merged and delivered same-day. Counsel would have the full transcript of the entire day in their hands almost as soon as they got back to their offices. O'Connor and Buchanan could be reading what I'd typed that day before I even got home.

Before I left the office I sent myself the full audio file of the case, which I'm not supposed to do — I wanted to listen to the bits that I missed. So after feeding Ollie and taking him for a quick walk down to the park to do his business, I poured myself a cup of noodles and put the audio on. I kept listening to that section with Andy and the catch in his voice.

I don't — I don't go out much.

*

The second day of the *Hsu vs Cronshaw* trial was to be the evidence of Lewis Cronshaw. I logged on, had a look over the log data, waited for another typist to take some of the boring stuff, and myself nabbed twenty minutes of audio right when Cronshaw came into the stand.

The little square of video appeared in the top right of my screen. It's only small, about 10cm squared, or maybe 15, and as I said, it's not the best quality — too brightly lit and too contrast-y, but you can make out a lot in that small space. The first thing I noticed about Cronshaw was that he seemed a lot more in control than Hsu. Hsu was slender and slight, hunched in the witness stand, Cronshaw was tall and well-built, with a straight bearing. He was wearing a blue suit and an open collared white shirt. He had on a pair of wire framed glasses and his hair was neat and tall, but clipped close on the sides. He only looked in his mid-30s. I'd expected someone older, someone crustier, something more like a predator. But this guy looked okay. He looked reasonable. But the picture was poor, it was hard to tell.

I paused the audio and went online, searched for pictures of Lewis Cronshaw. There were only a few online, and some of them were a lot clearer than the picture I had on my screen. There was a professionally taken portrait shot on the Steggle & Allan website, a shot taken against a white background. He was schmick and besuited, his suit sat perfectly on his shoulders, his tie was knotted neatly, his hair was perfect, his glasses perfect, his smile perfect. He wasn't attractive, as such, in fact he was a little ordinary looking, but something about how perfectly groomed he was gave him an air of being something special. He also looked supremely confident, direct and friendly. He looked like a nice guy. I think. His eyes — they looked — didn't they look kind?

None of this was doing anything for my word-count, so I got off the internet, pressed my pedal and started typing.

Mr O'Connor opened by taking Cronshaw through some really basic background information. His work history and his time with Steggle & Allan. He moved on to his social life, confirmed that Cronshaw identified as gay, didn't have a partner, and slept around — 'played the field' was the term used. He had in the past had sexual relations with men that he had met at work, twice in fact, before he had become interested in Andy Hsu. O'Connor then went deep behind enemy lines. He said that they had heard in court about Cronshaw's inappropriate behaviour in the workplace towards Mr Hsu, including looks that had been interpreted a certain way, comments, and inappropriate touching 'in the compactus'.

O'CONNOR, MR: You've heard these comments? - - - I have.

And while we all understand that you are not on trial here today because of inappropriate workplace behaviour, do you have anything to say about these inappropriate behaviours? - - - Yes, I do. I admit to all of them.

You admit to them? - - - I do.

You know that this behaviour is inappropriate? - - - I do.

He left that dangling and took Cronshaw back and over his entire interaction with Andy Hsu. When Hsu had started at Steggle & Allan, what had their working relationship been like? It had been, according to Cronshaw, very much a mentor and student working relationship to start with.

O'CONNOR, MR: And when did that change?

The way Cronshaw told it there had grown a mutual attraction between the two men. Although Hsu was not very communicative, Cronshaw felt he was indicating interest in other ways. What other ways? By hanging around his office, by lingering in the copy room or the compactus when he was around. He seemed to Cronshaw shy and reserved, but there had been smiles between them, there had been looks, and Cronshaw knew that Hsu had a crush on him.

HER HONOUR: You can't testify as to what was in another person's mind, Mr O'Connor — you know that. Let's steer clear of loaded looks from now on.

O'Connor and Cronshaw kept it more concrete. He asked Cronshaw how Hsu had reacted to these inappropriate workplace flirtations. Cronshaw said that when he had winked, or said something a bit risqué, or when he had 'touched' Hsu in the compactus that time, Hsu, said Cronshaw, had blushed and smacked his hand away — but he had not himself moved away. He had, said Cronshaw, smiled at him.

O'CONNOR, MR: And you took that to mean? - - - I took that to mean that he didn't mind — that he liked the flirtation.

From there they went on to the Friday night drinks. Cronshaw said that Hsu was quick to attend Friday night drinks when he, Cronshaw, had invited him, even though Hsu was more junior to the others going, and didn't drink alcohol.

O'CONNOR, MR: And you took that to mean? - - - I took that to mean that he was interested in me.

And at Friday night drinks did Mr Hsu participate in conversations? - - - To a degree, yes. He didn't have the same sort of knowledge of the business as the rest of us, and our talk was a bit boring, I suppose — a lot of work stuff. He often just sat there.

And did you and he talk at all on these occasions? - - - We did.

Under what circumstances? - - - When I would go to the bar, sometimes he would come along and stand next to me. We would talk then, a little.

He followed you around, in fact? - - - Well, it seemed like that, yes. He didn't go up to the bar when anyone else was getting drinks.

And what did you talk about when you were up at the bar? - - - Different things.

Did you make any propositions to Mr Hsu when you were out of earshot of the others? - - - I did.

And what was that proposition? - - - Well, I said — once I said — am I allowed to say …

I'm sure the court has heard it all before, Mr Cronshaw. Please speak freely? - - - I asked him when we were going to fuck.

You asked him when you were going to fuck. And what did Mr Hsu say to that? - - - He said we shouldn't. Then he blushed and turned away.

He did not take offence at what you said?

BUCHANAN, MS: Objection.

HER HONOUR: Move on, please, Mr O'Connor.

O'CONNOR, MR: And when you had purchased the drinks, what did he do? - - - He helped me carry them back to the table.

He didn't walk out — storm out of the bar and leave? - - - No.

And did he refuse to come along to Friday night drinks on subsequent occasions? - - - No, he would usually come along if I was going.

And you took that to mean? - - - I took that to mean that he wanted to sleep with me.

My audio ran out there, but I quickly grabbed some more, and got in later in Cronshaw's evidence. We had skipped ahead to the night in question. I listened to a bit to catch up. Cronshaw gave evidence about being out drinking with friends and being up for a big night out. But his friends had disbanded and gone home early, so instead of going on by himself he had got a taxi home. Then, on the way, remembering that he was going past Andy's street, he had asked the taxi to turn off and drop him out the front of Andy's flat. He admitted that he was drunk, he admitted that he was perhaps not thinking clearly. He even admitted that he had taken Andy by the arms and kissed him uninvited.

O'CONNOR, MR: And what did he say when you did that? - - - He couldn't say anything for a while, because my mouth was on his, but when he could he said no.

He said 'no'. Just that word? - - - Yes.

And what did you do? - - - I let him go immediately and we stepped apart.

How did you feel at that moment? - - - A bit mixed up.

A bit mixed up. What do you mean? - - - Well, I thought I'd got it wrong. I mean, got it wrong turning up late and drunk. I thought I'd messed things up, been too full-on for him. I was only concerned for him. I didn't want to upset him.

What did you do next? - - - I said I'd go. He said, yes, I should go. But I needed the toilet, so I asked if I could use it.

And you used it? - - - I did.

Here it was again — things were slowing down. Super-slow-motion. We went through the visit to the bathroom in detail.

And when you had finished in the bathroom, what did you do? - - - I came out back into the passageway and into the lounge room.

And where was Mr Hsu? - - - He wasn't there.

This was unexpected.

He wasn't there? - - - No. He wasn't in the lounge-room. I called his name, but there wasn't any answer.

And what did you do then? - - - I went back — I turned back and went back down the hallway. There's a door opposite the bathroom. It was open. And Mr Hsu was in bed.

Mr Hsu was in his bed? - - - Yes, he was. On the far side of the bed. The side nearest the door was free.

And what did you do? - - - I went in, and I undressed and I got in with him.

So that's how it happened, according to Mr Cronshaw. There were no pinioned arms, was no forcing of Andy Hsu into his bedroom. None of it. Here is where their two versions of events differed.

O'CONNOR, MR: And did Mr Hsu say anything at any time? - - - He said that we shouldn't do this. That we'd regret it.

I want you to be very clear. Did he say 'you' shouldn't do this, 'you' will regret it, or did he say 'we' shouldn't do this, 'we' will regret it? - - - He said we.

And what did you take that to mean? - - - I took it to mean he was nervous about it, and perhaps he was thinking about how it was inappropriate because we worked together, but ...

But? - - - But I took it to mean that he wanted to.

The rest of Mr Cronshaw's evidence was over pretty quickly. There was no need to go into too much detail about the sex according to Mr O'Connor. It happened, it was not particularly violent or, it seems, particularly passionate. It happened, and then, when it was over, Mr Cronshaw got up and left.

O'CONNOR, MR: Why did you leave? - - - Well, I wanted to get home.

I mean, perhaps, why didn't you stay? - - - I could see — I could tell Mr Hsu was …

Only what you saw and heard, please, Mr Cronshaw? - - - He lay with his back to me and didn't say anything. When I asked how he was he didn't answer. When I asked again he said he was okay. Then I left. I felt uncomfortable.

Did you feel as if you'd done something wrong? - - - No. No, I didn't feel that. I felt as if Mr Hsu felt he had done something wrong.

BUCHANAN, MS: Objection.

HER HONOUR: Over-ruled. Go on.

O'CONNOR, MR: And in the days following that evening — at work — what did you observe? - - - Mr Hsu wasn't in on the Monday following that night, but after that he was back in.

And what did you observe? - - - He was very upset.

Mr Cronshaw said it very matter-of-fact, but there seemed to be a host of meaning underneath his answer. According to Mr Cronshaw Mr Hsu came back to work on the Tuesday and from that day on he seemed to be avoiding him, Mr Cronshaw, altogether. He did not smile at him, he no longer hung around near him or came along to Friday night drinks. When he, Mr Cronshaw, had attempted to open conversation with Mr Hsu, he had been snubbed. When he, Mr Cronshaw, had attempted to laugh it off, joke about it, even apologise for it, he had been snubbed.

O'CONNOR, MR: Why did you want to apologise? - - - Because I knew …

As you know, Mr Cronshaw, you can't give evidence about what you think you know, only what you have seen or heard. Why did you want to apologise? - - - Because Mr Hsu seemed to be very upset, very hurt, and I was sorry for him. I was sorry. I wanted him to be okay with what had happened. I thought he was being too hard on himself.

Was your apology an admission of guilt? - - - No. No, it wasn't. I did nothing wrong.

*

I ate my sandwich in the park a block from work. I had now heard all the evidence on either side — from Andy Hsu and from Lewis Cronshaw. They had been in a courtroom just a few blocks from my park. They were now having lunch as well, the same as me, ushered out different doors, perhaps, and kept separate. The judge was in her chambers, working, presumably, on her summing up which was due the next day. Counsel were grabbing a quick sandwich, perhaps, or rapidly trying to source case law for some other case they were working on. This afternoon would be cross-examination of Mr Cronshaw by Miss Buchanan.

*

She went in on the attack. I think she realised she had to. If Mr O'Connor was playing around with the idea of consent, she would have to do the same. She began, quite strongly, I thought, with asking what Mr Cronshaw's idea of consent was. It was a line of questioning that couldn't go far — asking non-expert witnesses for opinions just wasn't done. And sure enough O'Connor got in an objection right up front. Miss Buchanan backed down immediately, which showed that question was more for general effect than evidence.

She went on to take Mr Cronshaw minutely over the interactions he had had with Mr Hsu, pointing out at each step of the way that never, ever, had Mr Hsu directly indicated an interest in Mr Cronshaw as anything other than co-worker, boss or mentor.

Her questions were long and involved and designed to cement the relationship between the two men in a certain light in the mind of the jury. Mr Cronshaw was rarely asked for more than a yes or no answer. Instead the questions positioned him as a man who had failed as a mentor, taken advantage of a young employee, eager and willing and naïve. Sometimes she got so involved in dissing Cronshaw via her questions, that she wound herself up into an impossible non-question, and had to just abandon it.

BUCHANAN, MS: And his deferral to you as the older man, the way he dogged your footsteps, the way he wanted to please, to do as he was told — couldn't all that be construed as nothing more than the relationship between a young lad and an older, more senior, much more experienced and confident man, a man who should be trusted with his position of power and authority — isn't that so? - - - I'm sorry, what's the question?

None of it was evidence, though, and the judge, after letting it run for a question or two to see where it was going, pulled her up on it.

HER HONOUR: You'll have a chance to address the jury presently, Miss Buchanan. Can I ask you to keep your questions to the point for the moment, please?

But the scene had been set. The questions could now proceed in a more appropriate fashion. Miss Buchanan ignored much of the detail — it seemed that much of the detail was now taken as read — and instead concentrated on the few moments that Mr Cronshaw had, in his previous evidence, expressed a slight sense of confusion or regret.

She drove her questions into those little crevices, and wriggled them around. She revisited the moment Hsu had said 'no' to the uninvited kiss, and Cronshaw said he had felt — what was it, she asked, 'mixed up'? What was it he was mixed up about? Was he confused about whether he had done the wrong thing? The right thing? Anyone might have doubts, self-doubts, in that moment. Cronshaw was almost drawn, it seemed, but then, as if remembering a lesson, remembering the 'right' answer, he said those few words that every cross-examining counsel must dread. 'I can't recall,' he said.

Ms Buchanan moved to the moment Cronshaw had left Hsu in the bed, his back turned. How had he felt then, at that moment? But he said it again. 'I can't recall,' he said again. Miss Buchanan changed tack slightly.

BUCHANAN, MS: And when you sought to apologise to Mr Hsu in the workplace in the week following the incident — did you feel a sense of guilt? - - - No. I had done nothing wrong.

You can feel a sense of guilt without doing anything wrong. Here was a young man, naïve and in your care, to a degree, who was now feeling very mixed up, very unhappy, all because of actions of yours — or actions you had encouraged him to take. Did you feel a sense of responsibility for him feeling the way he did? - - - Yes.

A sense of compassion? - - - Yes.

A sense of guilt? - - - No.

She wasn't going to crack him, but she didn't need to. Her line of questioning went on and on, and no matter what Cronshaw answered, he was positioned as a man who had abused a position of trust and responsibility, seduced a young and naïve man in his employ, felt remorse and compassion and regret for what he had done, and had in fact attempted to apologise for it.

It was as if the actual mechanics of the seduction no longer mattered, and in a way I guess they didn't. There was no use taking more evidence about whether or not Mr Hsu was taken forcibly into the bedroom, or lay in the bed waiting for Mr Cronshaw. It was the word of two witnesses against each other — he said / he said. And if she went down that track, rehashed that part of the evidence, it would only result in her own client looking bad.

Miss Buchanan wrapped up quickly, having done her best to place Cronshaw in a bad light, and without actually addressing very much evidence at all. It seemed to me that her tactic was rather a last-ditch one. It stank of a cross-examination without real purpose other than good old-fashioned mud-slinging. I wonder if the jury thought the same, and I wonder if they, like me, came to the same thought: the case against Cronshaw was on shaky ground.

O'Connor had made many points about Hsu not actually refusing consent, and in fact the term 'implied consent' had been bandied around a bit — enough to lodge in the minds of the jury. Plus, the jury, as I'm sure the judge would remind them, did not have to find Cronshaw pure as the driven snow, just guilty or not guilty — it wasn't the same thing.

Judge Macindoe adjourned the court and the second day of the trial was over.

I was so far behind in my word count because I'd listened to so much audio that wasn't mine to type, that I had to rush through a few unrelated jobs to get it back up, before logging off and heading home.

*

That night I woke at some time in the middle of the night, convinced that someone was in my flat. I wasn't sure what I'd heard, but something had woken me up. I listened hard, but I could hear nothing. Just the sound of the fridge, and the sound of little Ollie at the end of the bed, with his slightly asthmatic night-breathing.

No footsteps, no movement at all. I watched the door to the bathroom from my pillow. Watched for shadows. For movement. If he appeared at my door, a silhouette in the dark, would I shift over and make room for him?

*

The next morning I called in sick. I had decided to go to the court to see the summing up. And I wanted to see him. I wanted to see Lewis Cronshaw.

I contemplated taking Ollie, because I hadn't slept well, I was all over the place, and this felt like an Ollie emergency. He's allowed everywhere with me, pretty much, if I take the paperwork around saying he's a companion dog. But I didn't want him in court — people would look at me, and I couldn't face being stared at, not today.

I got the train in, got a coffee at Espress-n-go, and instead of turning to the office, I went straight ahead to the County Court. I'd looked at the times of the trials online, and of course, I knew when Judge Macindoe had asked for court to reconvene this morning, so I knew I was in plenty of time. In fact, I'd have to wait around a little, possibly.

I was out the front of the court, watching lawyers and legal aides walking back and forward with their big flapping black gowns, when I noticed, down the side street, a whole lot of news cameras, cameramen and photographers. As I approached a car drew up and three people got out. They came around the car to the back door closest to the building and opened it. A man got out, a man in a blue suit with a quiff of hair and glasses.

I moved forward, shouldered through the people. I wanted to see him. He was being shepherded forward through the cameramen. His companions weren't police, they didn't seem official at all — just friends or something, work colleagues from Steggles, or counsel or what? He had his head down and his eyes on the ground, not in a hang-dog way, but just as the easiest way to avoid the cameras. He seemed, otherwise, confident and in control.

One of the cameramen was in his way, which brought him up short. He lifted his head and he looked right at me. I saw his eyes, and I saw that I was wrong, that they weren't kind at all. I mean, they were at first — well, more blank than kind — but as he looked at me, just for that moment, I saw something in those eyes. I saw — and it's hard for me to describe it, because I'm not good at reading people — I saw a flicker, as if he had recognised me.

But I'd never seen the man before. I was sure of it.

It took me a moment to click that perhaps he recognised not my face, but something else. Did he recognise — bear with me because this is very awkward and odd for me — did he recognise not my face but something in me, something intrinsic? It felt like he saw — was it my Asperger's? Maybe. No. It felt like he saw and understood that I was vulnerable.

That's it. He looked at me as if he knew I could be fucked with.

It was only a second, but I felt it. I felt it.

And then his eyes changed again, they went blank and back down to the footpath. He stepped around the cameraman in the way and disappeared inside.

It wasn't evidence — it definitely wasn't evidence — *objection, Your Honour* — but I knew that he had done it. His version of the story wasn't the right one. Andy's version, as imperfectly told as it was, was the truth. I knew it.

*

As it turned out I didn't see or hear the judge's summing up or the jury's verdict that day. I didn't go into the court — I just couldn't do it, not after eyeballing the accused outside. And I'd already called in sick to work, so I couldn't go in there. I did, though, find the audio on the server the next day, and send it to myself, then listened that night.

O'Connor's final statement had been brief, but quite masterful. He knew he didn't need the jury to believe Cronshaw a knight in shining armour to get a not guilty verdict, and he played up on this.

O'CONNOR, MR: We do not dispute that Mr Cronshaw went to Mr Hsu's house in the early hours of the morning of the day in question. We do not dispute that he was drunk. We do not dispute that sexual relations took place. We do not dispute that Mr Hsu put in a sexual harassment claim at Steggles & Allan Legal a full two months after the event. We do not dispute that Mr Hsu has since been receiving psychiatric treatment due to not coping in the weeks after the events of that night. Let me make it clear — we do not dispute any of the evidence put before you by counsel for the prosecution. None of it.

He repeated himself a few times, driving his point home.

O'CONNOR, MR: The only thing we dispute is that Mr Cronshaw forced himself on Mr Hsu. The only thing we dispute is that Mr Hsu, in any way, via his actions or his words, made it absolutely clear to Mr Cronshaw that his attentions were not wanted, and that led Mr Cronshaw to make the assumption — yes, an assumption — that his attentions were wanted.

And then he laid it on the line.

O'CONNOR, MR: You must find Mr Cronshaw not guilty if there is any reasonable doubt in your minds that what occurred here was in fact statutory rape. Any - reasonable - doubt.

It seemed he'd saved all his bombastic pauses up for the end. It was simplistic, but it was effective.

Miss Buchanan came out swinging, with more of her verbose, rolling sentences designed to instil a certain picture of the accused in the mind of the jury. But it was too late for this and she moved on from it fairly rapidly. She bravely took the fight into enemy territory and challenged O'Connor's point about 'implied consent'.

Buchanan's point was that you could not, by the nature of consent, imply it — the only thing you could imply from an absence of consent was in fact non-consent. She had a point, perhaps, morally, but it was debatable whether or not it was a point of law.

The judge's summing up was scrupulously fair, of course, but must have been cold comfort for Miss Buchanan and Mr Hsu, for at every turn she reminded the jury that they were to consider only points of law, and what was said and done, not what may have been inferred or meant. With that summing up, fair as it was, there was really only one outcome, and it was as expected.

*

Was there consent or wasn't there? I don't know. All we can know, really, is that the court found in Cronshaw's favour, and that's not about whether or not there was consent, it's about whether or not there was evidence. I thought during this trial that I had taken good measure of Andy Hsu and of Lewis Cronshaw, but maybe I was wrong. The catch in Andy's voice at the start of his evidence, the look of the predator in Cronshaw's eye outside the court that day. How can I trust myself to be hearing it right, seeing it right? How do I know that what I interpreted is correct? Given my condition, given my past, given my *flaws*, wouldn't it be more likely that I was getting it wrong?

You know, it's occurred to me more than once that maybe the law is kind of like Asperger's. Obsessed by detail, but only able to draw certain prescribed conclusions from those details. Able to see, but unable to freely interpret. Blind to nuance. Blind to emotion. Blind, in the end, to truth.

If the law is like Asperger's, then maybe my head is like my typing — the emotion, the catch in the throat, the look in an eye, it's all missed out somehow, it's edited out and replaced by an emdash.

Maybe my life is a transcript, just words and dashes and punctuation. No context.

*

It was a week or more before I stopped searching the internet for news about the *Hsu vs Cronshaw* case, stopped stalking them on social media — neither of them were posting in the aftermath of the trial anyway. Oh, there were other bits and pieces. I'd had more dreams about home invasions, more dreams where I thought there was someone in the doorway watching me. I went down a bit of a rabbit-hole researching the law around consent. All sorts of things. But eventually these things ran their course and my mum came around and reminded me that I had to eat and shower regularly, and I was rid of it, rid of them, Hsu and Cronshaw. Rid of them and waiting for the next case to come along. Because — and this is full disclosure time — I admit that this is not the first time I have become obsessed like this about a case I am typing. It's not the first time, and I very much hope that it won't be the last.

You see, it's those days in between the obsessions that are the hardest. It's in those cracks that, with nothing else to think about, things come rushing into my head. How small my life is, how lonely I am, how cramped my little bedsit is. On days like these, there is only one thing to do, and that is to call in sick, call Ollie up onto the bed (he has his own little set of carpeted steps on his side), settle him into a nest of soft blankets right by my shoulder, and go back to sleep.

SALT

The landscape we were driving through was flat and scrubby, with occasional salt plains where water, in winter, had laid in shallow sheets, but had now, in summer, disappeared, leaving dead-flat salt-white expanses that stretched off to the horizon. I had come this way many times with my family and by myself, through the salt plains of the Coorong, to our family shack down the limestone coast. I had always, as a kid, wanted to walk in this moonscape, but my dad had not allowed it, so as soon as I was down this way under my own steam, as a P-plate driver, many years ago now, I stopped the car, got through the fence and gave it a go. The salt-white layer was thin and instantly crackled and crumbled to mud underneath — very smelly mud. Vile mud. So much so that I had to take my shoes off and do the rest of the drive barefoot, with my shoes in the boot.

My passenger was a hitchhiker, a familiar type in Australia — over-tanned legs and arms, with white-blond shaggy hair, perhaps stiff from the sea, and a backpack the size of a small car with bedrolls and shoes and all sorts attached to it. I'd picked him up just outside of Tailem Bend, an hour out of Adelaide. He was standing in the white dirt beside the road, just beyond the turn off from the main highway onto the smaller highway that went down directly along the coast.

I was on the way to the southern end of the Coorong, to a place called Cape Jaffa. A friend of the family spent time down there every now and then when he had to dive on Margaret Brock Reef to monitor the local rock lobster population. I was planning to join him for a few days R&R. It was a three-and-a-half-hour drive from Adelaide, and I still had two and a half of those hours to go when I picked him up at the side of the road.

I rarely picked up hitchhikers. In Australia, I think we're just about immune to thumbs out on the side of the road. There have been too many movies, too many real-life headlines about the dangers of hitchhiking. Even so, every now and then I picked up a hitchhiker like this one, a lone traveller, because I'd backpacked around myself when I was young, and I knew how much a good experience on the road could make or break your day. I liked to think, what with some good chat and not being a serial killer, that I was a good experience.

I stopped ahead of him, looked in the rear-view mirror and watched him haul his backpack onto one shoulder and shuffle-run towards the car. He came to the front door, dipped his head and said, 'Thanks, mate', through the open passenger-side window without making eye-contact with me. I said he could chuck his backpack in the back seat, so he did, then he came back, slipped into the passenger side seat and we drove off.

He was a young guy, only in his early 20s, I guessed, and while on the side of the road he had the look about him of a Scandinavian tourist, it was obvious once he got into the car that he wasn't. He didn't have the trace of an accent to start with. In fact, his 'mate' sounded completely and authentically Aussie, country-town Aussie, natural and throw-away. And there was something non-communicative and wound-up about him that I associated more with a local than with a tourist.

He was wearing short shorts, a button up short-sleeved khaki shirt, a massive black watch on a skinny wrist, and those very weird shoes that have separate toes to them — like gloves for your feet. As soon as he got in the car, I noticed he had a smell about him, like sweat and dirty hair, but old, as if he'd smelled like that for a while, maybe slept it in.

Even though he hadn't looked at me once, I could see he had light blue eyes, a little protuberant, a large strong-boned nose, and teeth that stuck out a bit so that his lips never quite closed over them. He was skinny, and his neck was long, with a strongly defined Adam's apple. He was quite tall and he sat with his back curved, his knees together and his hands folded over a notebook on his lap, spiral bound, with a pen jammed into the spiral.

I asked him how far I could take him, and he countered by asking how far I was going. I told him Cape Jaffa and he seemed to know of it. He nodded and said Cape Jaffa would do. He had, he said, no specific destination in mind, but wanted to keep moving around the coast.

'You're travelling around Australia then?' I asked him.

He shrugged.

'I've just started, really.'

'Where have you come from?'

'Tailem Bend.'

Tailem Bend? The town I'd just come through.

'So, you're just leaving now?'

'Yep. Just now.'

'How long were you waiting there at the corner?'

'A while,' he said, then he shrugged again as if something had just occurred to him. 'Not that long, really. I'm not sure how long you usually have to wait. You're my first.'

Overall, I have to say that after those first few minutes or so, the stink of him, the awkwardness of him, his weird eyes, the fact he wouldn't look directly at me, the fact he was from Tailem Bend, I wasn't sure whether I should have picked him up after all.

*

I don't remember how long we'd been driving before I asked him about the notebook on his lap. I guess it had to have been a while. I know that after we got underway I asked a few questions — nothing much, just a few simple chatty questions. But he answered with dead-end statements, usually just 'yep' or 'nup' if he could get away with it, or 'nuthin much' or 'don't know' if he couldn't.

I found my eyes going around to his profile again and again. Everything poked forward, and I could see the irises of his eye, side on, almost as if they floated on the white. There was something about his face, his weird eyes, the way he sat so intently focused on the road ahead that was slightly unsettling.

Even with the wind drumming through my open window, every now and then I got a whiff of him. There was something strange about the smell of him, as if he was sweating something nasty out of his system. Large patches of sweat had started to spread under his arms and in the neck of his shirt. His hair was darker around his hairline, and on his upper lip, protruding over those sticky-out teeth, there were little beads of sweat. Once or twice he raised his arm and wiped his mouth on his shoulder, leaving little wet patches on his shirt. I wondered whether it was fear he stank of, and if it was, what he was afraid of.

'Do you want me to turn on the aircon?'

'Nah,' he said. So I didn't.

Instead I told him about my friend, Mick, down at Cape Jaffa, and the fact he was a diver for Fisheries, and that he was down there counting the rock lobsters. That killed ten minutes. Then I asked about the notebook on his lap.

'What's in the notebook,' I asked.

I knew I'd hit on something. It was the first time he'd looked at me since he got in the car. His head turned and his too-light eyes swivelled to me and looked dead at me for a moment, just a moment, before he turned back. With that glance I knew two things about him. Yes, he was scared — of what? Why? — and also, he was a lot younger than I'd thought. He wasn't early 20s, he was younger than that, I was sure — still a teenager. A kid. It was all in those eyes, and in that look — wary, suspicious, with an overlay of youthful bravado.

'Nuthin,' he said.

'There's got to be something in there.'

He sat for a second, looking straight ahead again.

'Just stories,' he said, and he said it clipped and dismissive to downplay it.

'Stories? Like, stories you've written?'

He nodded.

'What sort of stories do you write?'

He shrugged.

'Fiction?' I asked.

'Yep.'

'I'm a writer, too,' I said. I'm not sure what encouraged me to say it, to confess it, as I did. I had not thought of myself as a 'writer' for many years now, so long that it seemed like a lie.

He turned to me again, less wary this time.

'Will I know you?' he asked.

'You might.' I told him my name and the name of my first book, but when I looked around there was not a flicker of recognition in those light eyes.

'Oh yeah,' he said, obviously never having heard of either before.

'I'm not surprised you don't know it,' I said. 'It was written about twenty years ago now. Made into a movie. Won an award.'

'Right,' he said.

His one word dismissal of my writing career seemed totally appropriate. It had been, when it happened, like fireworks going off one after the other - publication, a literary award, a movie adaptation, a three-book deal. It had felt like success and my future seemed assured. But the second novel, which had been so much harder to write, did not find the same audience — no award, no movie. And the third? Well, I had never completed the third and had to find a proper job to pay back the advance.

'What about your stuff?' I asked, turning the conversation away from my past and back to him. 'What do you write?'

'Science fiction, mostly,' he said eventually.

'Nice,' I said. 'Are you working on something now?'

'Yeah,' he nodded, with less enthusiasm.

'What?'

Like every writer talking about ideas, he was, to begin with, dismissive of them, belittling, and rather incoherent when he tried to describe them.

'Well, it's set in, like, the future,' he began.

'Right.'

'And in the future, it's, like, the worst possible future.' He looked at me then, with a little wince, as if embarrassed at how inarticulate he was. 'I'm not very good at describing this. It's better when I write it.'

'You could read it to me, if you want.'

He contemplated that for a second, and he even went so far as to move the notebook around on his knees, but then he seemed to think better of it.

'Nah. It's not — I haven't even really written anything much down. I've just — it's just notes really.'

We lapsed into silence. He lifted his arm and wiped his sleeve across his cheek and his mouth and, after another crafty half-look at me, he stared straight ahead again.

After a few more minutes I asked: 'So, does this story have a title?'

'Nuh,' he said.

'Characters?'

'Well, yeah, but not with, like, names or anything. Not yet.'

'An opening scene?'

'Actually yes,' he said, almost reluctantly. 'That's the one thing it does have, really.'

'And that is?'

He swallowed. I could see his Adam's apple bobbing up and down in his throat.

'It opens in a grove of trees,' he said.

I wound up the window to cut out the wind noise, and turned the aircon on.

'Go on,' I said.

He looked at me again, looked as if he might be losing his nerve, but then he opened his notebook and read me the opening scene of his story. It wasn't all that extraordinary as a concept, and I know that the words themselves, the sentences, weren't brilliantly crafted — they were, in fact, more like notes for an opening scene rather than an opening scene — but what he described has stayed with me ever since. Perhaps this is more to do with the circumstances, with what was to come after, I don't know — but I have never forgotten the image he described or the moment he described it.

'The story begins in a grove of trees,' he read. 'The trees are planted close together and in rows. Perhaps it is a plantation. But it doesn't seem like a plantation because there are different types of trees planted all together, different but with one thing in common, they are all deciduous. The trees are tall and mature. There is a thick canopy overhead and lush grass underneath. The sky above is black, because it is night, but the entire grove is floodlit by enormous banks of lights from outside the grove and amongst the trees. There are butterflies and bees and birds, active, confused by the lights. There are also many people amongst the trees. Some people are having picnics, some are strolling. There are young couples, happy and in love and holding hands. There are others, alone, wandering among the trees, looking up at the canopy, touching the trees as they walk past. There are so many people, quite a crowd of them. But no-one talks much. They seem to be waiting for something.'

'And then it happens. A countdown from ten starts, at the same time, from different parts of the crowd, just like on New Year's Eve. At the last shout of the countdown there is silence. Complete silence. Everyone is still, looking up. Then, there is a shudder. It gently jolts the foliage, and can be felt in the ground beneath them. A shudder and then a jolt. Then, after a moment or two, a breeze blows through the grove, a chilly breeze. Some of the people close the collars of their shirts, or pull on light cardigans they have with them. And then, slowly at first, we begin to see it. The leaves above them begin to change colour, from green to yellowy-green, to golden. It happens all at once, as they watch, right in front of their eyes. The first leaf falls perhaps a minute, no more, after the jolt. Two or three people try to catch it. It is considered good luck to catch the first leaf, like a bride's bouquet. Someone does. A young man. He gives it to his girlfriend. Then another leaf falls, and another, and then, all at once, the rest of the leaves fall. It is a great dump of leaves. Heavy and thick. In seconds the trees are completely bare. Every leaf has fallen. Every single leaf. The people under the trees, some of whom, those sitting on picnic blankets, are virtually buried to their necks in autumn leaves, all the people give a great whoop as one, a gigantic cheer.'

He stopped reading, closed the notebook and looked warily at me, waiting for my reaction, trying to assess, seconds before I could say anything, what I thought, what my reaction might be. He looked ready to jump either way, depending on what my reaction was, ready to break into a big goofy grin if I said I liked it, or come out fighting and snarling if I said I didn't.

'I love it,' I said, and he broke into the expected grin, revealed the gums around his sticky-out teeth. He blushed a little, and looked confused and excited.

'It's really rough, I know,' he said taking the expected turn into self-deprecation. 'But thanks.'

I had experienced this sort of thing in the past when working with young writers, giving feedback on manuscripts. That first moment of vulnerability, a feeling that I had their lives in my hands, almost, and that my next words could send them either shooting up like a firework or spiralling down into deep wells of despair. I had been like that about my writing when I was young — touchy, needy, unsure. I can't feel like that any longer. After so many contradictory opinions and reviews, there's no point in listening to them any longer, good or bad. The bad no longer stings, I admit — you can say what you like, criticise as much as you wish — but unfortunately the positive doesn't thrill like it used to either.

I could never, of course, have remembered precisely the words that he used to describe the grove of trees and what happened there if it was just a question of memory. The conversations I've written here, they are as accurate as I can make them. I know we said something like that, and I have tried to be as true as I can to the conversation we had. But, as it turns out, I don't have to rely on my memory of the words he used to describe the grove of trees, because I have his notebook, the one he read from, here with me now, right beside me on the desk. It is easy to read and easy to transcribe. His handwriting is clear and neat, and that as much as anything else gives away his extreme youth. It looks like the hand of a schoolboy.

*

'Is there more?' I asked.

'More?'

'Of your story. Are you going to read any more to me?'

'Well,' he said. 'I'm afraid that's all I've written so far.'

I was disappointed. That was not so much a story as a circumstance.

'I was hoping there would be more.'

146

'Well, there is more. There's a lot more. I just haven't written it yet.'

'Can you tell me about it?'

'Okay,' he said, then sat contemplating the road ahead for a minute.

'Would it help if I asked questions?'

'Okay. Yes. Good idea. Go ahead.'

'You said this story was set in the worst possible future, right? So my first question is: what sort of worst possible future is it? Terminator style, or just regular everyday global warming style?'

'Global warming style,' he answered readily.

'The sea levels have risen?'

'It's gone way beyond that. Like, there's no atmosphere on earth any longer. There's no air, there's no water, there's no plants. It's just — imagine the photos you've seen of the surface of the moon, or any other planet — just silt and rocks and black skies. It's a completely dead planet.'

'Right,' I said. 'Grim.'

'Yeah,' he said.

'But presumably there are pockets of life. The grove of trees. The people.'

'They live in a globe.'

'A globe?'

'They're all over the surface of the planet. In every — well, not in every country perhaps, but on every continent, maybe — I haven't really confirmed all the details, yet — there are globes, and inside the globes it's like a greenhouse.'

'Got it.'

'And each globe is the size of — I don't know, but it's big enough to house a whole range of plants and animals. As big as a city, as big as a whole jungle. There are globes that cover rainforests and deserts and even a part of Antarctica. There are globes that are like massive aquariums, where sea creatures are kept — everything. Whole ecosystems are under these globes. And they're kept, the people and the plants and the animals — they're kept in artificially created atmospheres.'

'So they — whoever they are — turn on the seasons at the flick of a switch?'

'Yeah. That's it. And that's what's happening in the grove. They switch on autumn at midnight on the last day in February in that globe — it's in the southern hemisphere, here in Australia — and those trees, because they've been under a dome so long, they've changed, they've evolved, and now, when they sense the change in atmosphere, they instantly drop their leaves.'

'It's a beautiful image,' I said. 'And I can see the whole setup, actually. A dead planet. A black sky. And here and there pimples of lush green, of blue, or cityscapes, with, maybe, a bit of condensation on the globes.'

'Yes. I hadn't actually thought about condensation on the globes, but I'll write that down if you don't mind.'

I said that I didn't mind, and he took the pen out of the bindings of his notebook, flipped it open and scribbled a few words in the margin. He held his pen awkwardly and pressed too hard, like a child who is learning to write.

'So, anyway,' he went on unprompted when he was done. 'The story takes place in one single globe.'

'The one with the grove of trees.'

'Yes. It's a globe that covers a part of a city and a large bit of countryside. The people who live in that globe, a lot of them were born in the globe and don't know anything about life before the globe. Most of the people, in fact. There might be one or two older people who remember life before the globes, but there aren't, actually, a lot of older people around. It's mostly younger people, people of child-bearing age. And children. Children and adolescents and young parents, that's it. They know the history — I mean, the creation of the globes and the death of the planet. It's done in history in schools. So everyone knows that there are globes all over the surface of the planet, but they've never seen them. They never leave their own globe. The world outside is a complete unknown to them.'

'Sounds suspicious.'

'It does, doesn't it?' he said with a smirk.

'So, what happens next?'

He seemed flummoxed by such a direct question, so I backpedalled. Obviously he'd worked out the story without working out how it unfolded scene by scene.

'What about characters? Can you tell me about the characters in the story?'

'Sure. Yes, I can. There are five characters.'

'Five. Got it.'

'I don't have names for them, like I said. There's a pregnant woman, a childless couple.' He hesitated for a second there, giving me side-eye again. 'And a gay couple.'

'Right. I begin to see.'

'Do you?'

'Sort of,' I said.

'There are very strict rules, right. Because there is such a small population in the globe, there's no such thing as a love match any longer. Young people of child-bearing age, they're told who it is safest to have a child with, genetically, and they are required to keep trying for a child until they get one of the desired sex — gender. Anyone who cannot have children, any infertile people, or people who are unwilling to have a child with the partner chosen for them — they are outcasts and they are sent away. You get it?'

'I'm following,' I said. 'And your five characters are outcasts?'

'Yes. One, the pregnant woman, she's pregnant with a baby of the incorrect gender and she refuses — she won't have an abortion. The childless couple, they've fallen in love, but they are not an agreed child-bearing match and so are expected to partner with others. The gay couple — well, of course, they are also outcasts.'

He was on a roll now. Staring straight ahead, straight down the road. If I looked at him I could see his weird too-light irises apparently floating on the whites of his eyes, his protruding top teeth coming down on his bottom lip to make 'b' sounds, and a bit of spittle, like a white dot, forming at the side of his mouth; his Adam's apple bobbing up and down in his throat as he spoke and swallowed.

'So yeah, that's the story. The five outcasts, they want to break free of this — like, this oppressive prison they're in. They want to get out of the system, break out of the globe, escape and live the life they want to live. So they make their plans, and they meet in the grove. Then, on the stroke of autumn, under cover of the crowds, under cover of the dump of autumn leaves, they break away and they head towards the escape-pod.'

'The escape-pod? This is new.'

'Well, it's not called an escape-pod. It's called — actually, I don't know what it's called. It's really just, like, a surface jeep, like a moon buggy almost. It's larger though, like a Hummer-limo, a Hummer-moon-buggy-limo, and it's used — well, everyone in the globe is told that it's used to transport people from one globe to another when other globes need new blood for safe breeding. But these five outcasts, they've talked about this, and they don't believe that, because they never get an incoming Hummer-limo of new people. It's always people from their globe leaving and never coming back. And it's usually outcasts like them, or older people past child-bearing age, that are taken out of the globe. But the outcasts, they suspect that these people, they're not taken to other globes. Not really. They suspect they're taken out onto the surface of the planet,' he said slowly. 'They're taken out and they're just left to die out there.'

'I see.'

It was at this point that I started to feel a renewal of my unease from earlier.

The drive to that point, as a drive, may as well not have happened. After winding up my window to cut out the drumming of the wind, I don't remember another single moment of the mechanics of the drive — the road, the landscape, the other cars, slowing down for corners, indicating to overtake, anything — I remember nothing except this boy and his story. But then, at that moment, when he talked about outcasts being taken out on the surface of the planet and left to die, I became suddenly aware of how alone we were on the road, not a car as far as the eye could see before or behind us, and how those vast salt plains stretched off either side towards the horizon, with only a little bit of scrub here and there to break the surface.

Yes, he had relaxed somewhat, had gone from monosyllabic to talkative, but I thought back to when he had got into my car, silent, full of nerves, coiled like a spring, sweating and reeking of fear. Yes, he seemed thoughtful and even poetic in his imaginings, but he was also, wasn't he, just a little bit unhinged? Yes, he was just a young kid, but he was also gangly and tall and his hands were big. There was a sense of strength about him. A sense that he was a fighter. I noticed that the knuckles on his right hand were grazed and were starting to bruise. I'm not sure why I hadn't noticed before — perhaps the bruising had only just begun coming up.

I thought back to picking him up at the side of the road just outside Tailem Bend where, according to him, he had only just started hitchhiking. What was his story? What was back in Tailem Bend? What had he stepped away from back there before he got in my car and started telling me this story of air-conditioned snow-globes and Hummer-limo-moon-buggies, about outcasts being left to die?

'These outcasts,' I asked. 'Do they make it to the escape-pod? Do they get out?'

He shook his head, somewhat sadly, and then he shrugged.

'I don't know,' he said.

'You don't know?'

He shook his head again.

'I haven't written it yet, so I'm not sure which way it's going to go. I mean, I know that yes, they get in the Hummer-limo-moon-buggy and they drive out onto the surface of the earth. I'm just not sure what they find there, you know? Maybe there aren't any other globes out there after all. Maybe there were, but over the years those other globes have broken down. Maybe they cracked and the atmosphere seeped out. Maybe there were uprisings — other people, in the other globes, maybe they revolted and there were fights, wars even. Maybe animals were unable to live in the globes? Maybe plants, crops, everything failed? Maybe this one globe, the one with the grove of trees, maybe that's the only one left operating, and they're just living on there, year after year, without knowing they're the only one. The seasons switch over automatically every three months, but there's no-one left running it, and there's nowhere left out there to go.'

'That's your end?'

He sat for a minute.

'No,' he said. 'Well, yes, I think it is. But I want to make it — I want to write it in a way that it seems hopeful.'

'Driving out onto a dead planet?'

'Yeah,' he said. 'You know?'

And I did know. I think I did.

'Like, they head out,' he went on, 'and even if there isn't anything there, no air, no water, no atmosphere, and even if there are no other globes left, even if there is absolutely nothing out there, it's better than what they've got inside the globe, you know? It's certain death, yes, but it's also self-determination.'

'I see.'

I nodded for a bit. And then I gestured to his bruised knuckles.

'What happened in Tailem Bend?' I asked him.

He turned to look at me then, and his weird light-blue eyes were impossible to read.

'That's another story,' he said.

'Does that one have a happy ending?'

'Yeah,' he said. 'Me in this car.'

Because of course he was a runaway, and I was aiding and abetting him.

*

I found his notebook weeks later under the passenger side seat. I don't remember seeing it slip off his lap, but it could have done, perhaps at some point when he was especially enraptured by his own storytelling. I was, of course, paying attention to the road, and I might not have noticed. It could have slipped off and down the side of the seat and worked its way underneath. But if that was the case, how strange that he didn't realise when he got out. The way he kept it on his lap, with his hand over it, steadying it on his leg all through the drive — if the notes for the story he had told me, and any other notes he had in there, meant so much to him, as they seemed to, surely he would have realised when he got out of the car that he was missing it.

No, the notebook could only have been under the seat by design. He had slipped it under there himself. It's the only thing that makes sense. During the story, as my attention was on the road, at some point he had reached down between his legs and casually slipped it under the seat. Left it for me? Or just left it behind?

After reading the notebook through, the question he had never answered that day in the car, when I had asked him what had happened in Tailem Bend, was answered. There were other notes in there for stories, all of them written in his clear, legible, schoolboy handwriting, a mish-mash of science fiction ideas, dark and moody, all of them indicating a longing to escape — and in amongst these notes were sketches, diary entries. It was just him and his dad at home. It was a violent home. I won't go into too many details, because I'm sure he wouldn't want me to, if he's still out there, if he ever reads this, but it explains a number of things — the scrapes on his hand, the bruising, the fear, the intent focus on the road ahead. It also explains him leaving the notebook under my passenger side seat because, well, why wouldn't he want to leave all that behind?

I dropped him off at a petrol station at the turn-off to the dirt road down to Cape Jaffa. He lugged his backpack out of the back seat, hitched it onto his back, then he leaned on his bony forearms in the open passenger-side window.

'Bye,' he said, mopey and monotone, dead-eyed, as if none of his story had ever happened. 'Thanks for the lift.' And with that he turned and walked towards the petrol station.

As he walked away, I felt an odd lurch in my chest. I wanted to call out, call him back, but what for? I closed my eyes.

This boy, something about him, everything about him, had released inside me a memory, a feeling that the world out there was full of big skies, choose-your-own-adventure futures, and plenty of time to work out the next part of the story, that within me was a yearning to get out and grab it — an energy, a gravitational pull. I felt it — in my chest, in the hairs on my arms. I felt it. At the same time, in the same moment, I knew that I no longer had the capacity to feel it, not for real, and that my life was not a great unknown pull of possibilities, it was a known quantity, smaller and more defined than it had been last year, and the year before that, right back to my childhood when I had wanted to go out and walk on the salt plains.

When I opened my eyes he had disappeared, presumably into the petrol station. But maybe not. Maybe he disappeared into thin air.

BAIT AND SWITCH

All I wanted was a sweet distraction for an hour or two,
I never intended to do the things we've done.

The young man who had been followed into the bookshop had dark hair, cut with a fade up the back and sides but left long and unruly on top. He was skinny, with not a shred of fat on his frame. His skinny jeans rode low on his hips, his underwear rising above, and while he had a thick belt with studs on it through the loops of his jeans, his pants could have been pulled down with a short sharp tug, had anyone wanted to do so. He wore a vintage Bruce Lee teeshirt, and a blue hoodie over that with a white string pull-cord through the hood, both ends of which had been chewed. He was young, but the pimples at the side of his mouth were from a bad diet rather than adolescence. He looked as if he had not washed his hair or his clothes for some time, and yet there was a clean, slightly scrubbed look about his face — clear eyed, a little flushed in the cheeks, a little wet behind the ears. Really he was little more than a kid, brittle on the outside, but with a soft centre, not a million miles away from the school boy he had quite recently been.

The young man who had followed him into the bookshop was also thin, and had bad skin. He wore skinny jeans with rips in both knees, black boots and the ubiquitous hoodie, zipped up right under his chin. He had a hatchet sharp face and a number one clippered head. He also looked hard on the outside, but lacked the air of being soft in the middle. There was something sharper about him, something more wary and on edge.

They had walked into the bookshop at almost the same time, the one with the closely clippered head just a moment or two after the one in the Bruce Lee teeshirt. At first glance it might have seemed that they were together, given their similar look, but they did not acknowledge each other, and instead went to different areas of the shop. Bruce Lee went directly to the new release shelf and began browsing. He had no clue, it seemed, what was going on around him. Hatchet face, on the other hand, merely walked to a position behind Bruce Lee, where he could look through a gap in the shelves and observe from a slightly hidden vantage point. He picked up whatever was in front of him (in fact it was an adult colouring in book) and held it as if he was looking at it, but he did not. Instead he stared steadily through the gap in the shelves, a hyper-aware, hungry look about him.

*

Eli Jackman, the young man with the number one clipper job, was totally focussed on the man in the Bruce Lee teeshirt. He could only see the back of his head from where he stood, but he focused on the hair at the nape of his neck as he bent to read — so short, like shaving stubble — and he imagined it under his fingertips, the rasp of it, imagined it on his tongue. He felt electrified and turned on.

157

He put his hand in his hoodie pocket and fingered the stubby syringe there, ran his thumb down the needle and made sure that it was still firmly capped. It was. He had only done this twice before, and the thrill of it was still equally mixed with a burning fear it would go wrong, that the drug wouldn't work, that he would mess it up, that he would be caught, found out, arrested. It was odd, but even that thought, that string of thoughts, did nothing but make him more ardent, more excited. He wasn't quite sure where it had started, but this particular compulsion had been with him for some time — the need to have sex with someone without them knowing.

He had been a very shy child, awkward with other kids, prone to long bouts of silence alternating with extended spurts of energy. Once, when he was quite young, he had run around and around and around the house, faster and faster, cutting it finer and finer until he had started bashing his shoulder against the corners of the house and his mum had made him stop. He had, on the other hand, done exceptionally well at cross-country running as well as sprints at the school sports.

When puberty came it hit him like the corner of a house. It was year 9 and he began getting an erection at any random given moment and for, it seemed, absolutely no reason. He developed a crush on a variety of people at school, girls and boys and teachers. His lust, it seemed, was as generic as it was ardent. But aligned with this was a total inability to actually speak to people — more than that, a definite desire not to speak to people. And so, in order to satisfy his lusty thoughts, he took pleasure where he could, like a sneak-thief. Crowds became his outlet, the crowded school bus, lines at the school cafeteria, football scrums, anywhere there could be enough proximity that he could let an apparently casual hand brush against a leg, a bum, a breast, or even a boy's dick if he dared. It was usually a hand, but sometimes he also angled his pelvis in such a way, behind someone else in line, or on the bus, so that he could press his dick against them. There were, for a sneak-thief like him, plenty of opportunities in an over-crowded public school system.

As he got older girls became interested in him, as well as the odd boy — his moody aloofness had begun to work in his favour — and he went on a few conventional dates, but his complete inability to speak socially to people always did him in. On the few occasions where things progressed to physical affection, despite the lack of conversation preceding, kissing or feeling each other up, his body did not respond as he might have expected. He always shied away from actual sex, became prudish about it, and then angry and dismissive. It was an instinctive thing, an inability somewhere inside him to proceed. He couldn't stand to be looked at, he couldn't stand to be seen, spoken to, or touched. He wanted sexual fulfilment without any personal interaction at all, but that, of course, didn't seem to make any sense.

When he finally lost his virginity it was to an older girl, a woman really, who took him firmly in hand and pretty much did all the work herself. But even this didn't unlock anything inside him. He spent the entire time, his muscles rigid, his mind focused on trying to get through it, willing himself to stay hard and make it through to a satisfactory conclusion. Not for his pleasure, or for hers, but just for show, really, just so that it would be over.

During all this time, his libido did not relax. He still had an incredible appetite for sexual gratification. He began watching a lot of porn - masturbation became a regular pastime. When he was not watching porn, was out of the house, on the bus, on the street, he often found his mind wandering through intricate sexual fantasies, including men and women and all sorts of permutations.

He continued touching people up in crowded places whenever he thought he could get away with it. His touch was so careful, so soft, that he was virtually never discovered. There had been one or two times when he had gone a step too far — one time at a street corner in the city he had pressed up close to a fit young man in a white shirt and suit pants, carrying his suit jacket, waiting to cross, and he had, first, cupped his hand around one cheek of the man's buttock, then, with careful pressure, let his fingertips travel down and further in to the warmth between his legs.

The young man had spun around and looked at him with eyes at first wide and surprised and then hard and angry.

'Get your hand out of my arse, pervert,' he had said, without heat.

That had happened a few times, not many, and whenever it did Eli just stood his ground and acted nonplussed. It usually put whoever he had been touching on the back foot — had they been mistaken? — and defused the situation enough for him to get away with it. He found it was easier to get away with touching up men rather than women. Women, perhaps, had to be more vigilant, more willing to call out that sort of behaviour. Men, if he was careful, seemed mostly oblivious and clueless, and reluctant to believe an apparently accidental contact was intentional.

So it was that when Eli left high school and went to university to study engineering, he was, even in his own mind, a misfit, a pervert, a sociopath. He worried that one day he would go too far — knew, really, that he would, and wondered whether it would be the undoing of him.

*

Erik Simms, the young man wearing the Bruce Lee teeshirt, had no idea he was being watched by Eli. He left the bookshop without buying anything. He was really just killing time until his shift started. He had browsed through the new releases, and thought he could happily read some of them, if he could ever get around to actually reading fiction again. He didn't seem to read anything other than textbooks these days. He was in his final year of a double degree in humanities and psychology, working shifts in a commercial kitchen, and when he wasn't doing either of those things he was, it seemed, more and more of late, going out until the early hours of the morning, taking drugs or drink or a combination of both. Reading for pleasure simply did not feature, which he found a pity — he used to be such a bookworm as a kid. He had read all the childhood classics, *The Lion the Witch and the Wardrobe*, *The Hobbit*, *The Lord of the Rings*, the Harry Potter series, and, later, he and a group of girls in High School had even devoured the *Twilight* series and mooned over Edward and Jacob together. He'd read all the Bronte sisters, a bit of Dickens, a bit of Shakespeare, and re-read *Rebecca* by Daphne du Maurier every year. In his final two years of high school, having realised that he was gay (his *Twilight* girlfriends had worked that out already), he began a systematic reading of as much gay literature as he could get his hands on.

Reading had always meant so much to him. It had almost defined him. He missed it now, but with his new life it didn't feature as much as it once had. Perhaps he should have bought that gay novel he had seen back on the new releases shelf. He pulled up, considered turning back to buy the book, then looked at his watch — no, there was no time. His shift was due to start in 10 minutes.

Behind him, Eli stopped short at the same time Erik did and stepped sideways into the shadow of an awning in case he turned back.

What was he doing? Hesitating on the footpath like that? Did he realise he was being followed? But no, apparently not — he saw Erik check his watch and keep walking. After a moment, Eli stepped out of the shadows and did the same.

Erik walked on to the intersection, then stopped and waited with the others gathered there for the lights to change. He didn't notice Eli make his way through the pedestrians and stand directly behind him. Eli had risked coming up close behind him, within sniffing distance, touching distance — it was dangerous, given what he was planning, but pushing the boundaries was a part of what excited him. Erik, with his slender frame, did not have a perceptible curve to his bum, so there was nothing for Eli to brush his hand against, and he didn't bother making the attempt. He had a momentary desire to touch the exposed skin at the back of Erik's neck, instead, with the softest brush of his fingertips, but he forcibly restrained himself from doing so.

For many years Eli had fantasied that his touch, the very slightest touch of his skin against the skin of someone else, would render them totally in his power and amenable to his every whim, so that they would follow where he led, and do everything he wanted. Handshakes could do it, casual touches on the bare elbow could do it, but also, in his fantasy, more daring skin on skin contact would do it — if he slipped his hand inside someone's clothing on the street, touched a woman's breast inside her blouse, or if he grabbed a man's dick in the change-room — the shock and the anger would be nullified instantly as soon as the magic of his skin-on-skin touch took effect, and then the anger would change to blank-eyed acquiescence and they would do as he wished.

It was this, a sort of anonymous control, that he lusted after. As soon as the object of his desire saw him, locked eyes with him, divined his own interest, responded, either by recoiling or inviting, something was lost, something was gone, and it was that something that was the kernel of his desire. Without it he felt nothing.

Eli chanced blowing on the back of Erik's neck instead of touching the skin there, but just as he did so, the lights changed and Erik strode off across the road. Eli fell in behind him and followed him all the way to the restaurant where he worked in the kitchen. Eli had been here before, he had followed him here before. He knew when his shift started, he knew when his shift finished. He knew at what time of night he walked home, and down which streets.

*

Sex was not a big part of Erik's life. In fact, he hardly ever had it. His childhood hadn't been ideal — his dad had left when he was young, his mum was hardly ever around, and the uncle and aunt he'd been left with had mistreated him. This had left him, in his own words, a bit broken. Sex had not come easily the first time, and it had not been any easier since. He felt desire for other young men quite regularly. He could see a sharp profile on a train, or on the street, an Adam's apple, a skinny wrist (his tastes leaned towards skinny poetic types with floppy hair) and fall in love almost instantly. He had desire in him, a desire to find pleasure in company and intimacy, a desire to please, to take pleasure, and he wasn't, theoretically, opposed to any sexual act whatsoever — it was just that his body didn't cooperate. In fact, it recoiled. And he found that if things didn't go smoothly in the bedroom in the early stages, things rarely progressed to the latter stages. So, at 21 he had, if not sworn off men altogether, started avoiding potential embarrassment and rejection, which almost amounted to the same thing.

Even so, Erik was, deep down somewhere, in a naïve way, a hopeless romantic. He believed that out there, somewhere, was the man for him, someone who would love him and understand him, take him in hand and make it all just work. He was a bit unsure about how that man would ever find him, ever get past how broken he was, but he believed that somehow he, whoever he was, would.

When it happened — and it had only happened two and a half months ago, so it was only early days yet — it hadn't been at all how he'd thought it would be. Yes, there had been the Adam's apple, the sharp profile, the skinny wrists, there had been the sharp twinge of desire, but this young poet (a songwriter in fact) had been, if it were possible, even more broken than Erik was. And that, even if Erik couldn't quite make himself believe it was the healthiest thing on the face of the earth, had worked. Erik found in himself a feeling that he was needed, that he could help, a sense of empathy and purpose that he had never had before. He found that his own issues were no longer the elephant in the room, and that freed him up. His body, let off the hook, began to respond. In fact — and this made him smile to himself when he was on a train, or walking in the street, no longer taking a single bit of notice of anyone else — he had been the one to make the first move.

Stacking the commercial pass-through dishwasher, he thought of his new boyfriend, waiting at home, and a rush of love came over him, washed through him. All was right with the world when even someone like him could find someone to love.

When he finished work, some loads of dishes later, he threw off the apron, threw on his hoodie and left in a rush to get home. He didn't live far away, about a 15 minute walk, but he had to twist and turn down a few back streets, cross a park and cut along a walkway beside a railway line to get there in that time. If he went via the main streets it took more like 20 minutes, and he didn't want to waste five minutes of his life on the long way round.

At one point on his route, the end of a dead-end street abutted the path along the railway line. It was only a small street that serviced the back of a number of warehouses and private garages — it was not a residential street. There were, however, always a lot of cars parked up and down the street, as there were few restrictions and cars could be left there all day or all night. It was here, crossing the end of that dead-end street, that Erik noticed a car close-by had one of its back doors open. It was immediately after this that he saw in his peripheral vision a shadow close behind him. He felt a wiry arm circling him from behind, clamping his own left arm to his side, a body, legs, against the back of his own body as he was bent backwards and off balance. His one free arm flailed for a moment, trying to regain balance, but at the same time he felt a sharp pain in his neck, a needle-prick. He felt a shock of adrenalin, a spurt of fear, and he made a lunge away, against the arm, but adrenalin was followed, almost instantly, by a sense of calm, of acceptance, and then a tide of black rose up behind his eyes, and he lost consciousness.

*

Sex was not a big part of Eli's life either. In fact, he hardly ever had it. Once he worked out that it was anonymity and sexual control he craved, that didn't leave too many legitimate options open to him. He tried gay beats, gay sex on premises venues, which were, to a degree, anonymous, but he found that even there he was never really as anonymous as he craved, and certainly never totally in control — the very act of participating, even in role-playing S&M, was in itself consent. What he really craved was lack of consent. He craved, didn't he — there was really no other way to say it — he craved a very specific type of rape. And that was crossing a line — that wasn't a sexual fetish, it was a crime. It was wrong. But as much as he had deviated from the straight and narrow, he didn't think of what he lusted after as wrong. He didn't like to think of himself overpowering someone, assaulting someone, hurting someone, doing something wrong — and yet, that's precisely what he craved.

The closest he got to sexual satisfaction was when he got into the chemsex scene. He'd always been a casual drug-user. He'd drifted that way in the last year of school, first hanging out with the fringe-dwellers, boys who knew someone who knew someone who knew someone who sold drugs. Soon the degrees of separation were less. Soon after that he was selling them himself. He tried just about everything, but steered well clear of the harder stuff. Given the sort of person he was he didn't really like being out of control, and so being high didn't suit him in the least. He loved the power that drugs gave him, though, and he loved the way that other people, the drug-takers, were easier to manipulate when they were high. That, he thought, had a lot of promise.

At one point he had sold a party pack of drugs to an older man — fit but fucked up, he put it to himself — for a sex party, which included GHB, coke, MDMA, poppers, and to put a bow on it, Viagra. The man had then propositioned him, invited him along, and, curious, he had decided to go. The party had happened in Sydney at a massive apartment on the water over three levels with, the one time he cracked the blinds and let a bit of sunlight in, a view of the Bridge.

There was, at the height of the thing, about eight or nine men there, one of them in a wheelchair, but the number of participants ebbed and flowed. There was all sorts of sex going on, a lot of which he didn't participate in, a lot of which he wished he could un-see, to be honest, over all levels of the apartment. The whole thing went on for about three days, or maybe four — it was difficult to tell with the drug-taking and the blanked-out windows.

At one point he found one of the men passed out, naked, in a bedroom. Strangely, the bedrooms were the rooms least used for sex. He was not the man that had bought the drugs off Eli, but a type much like him, muscled and fit, but with a really old head on an apparently much younger body. Eli had grabbed his foot, waggled it, then, getting no response at all, slapped his exposed bum, white where his tan stopped — still there was no response. Eli climbed on top of him.

The sex, as far as Eli was concerned, was entirely satisfactory, even though the man's over-tanned skin slipped around on his muscles like it didn't fit. He was so excited he came in about five or six minutes, inside the man, and then immediately felt he could go again, and so did. It was all over in about a half hour. He was just about to leave the room when he came back, put the man on his side in the recovery position and checked his breathing. The man never regained consciousness throughout the entire thing and was, Eli presumed, completely unaware any of it had happened.

For a while chemsex parties were hitting the spot for Eli, and he was never short of an invitation given that he had the drugs, but eventually the appeal wore off. The sex he had at these parties, even if it was with men who were off their heads, or even like the first one, completely unconscious — it was consensual, for the very simple reason that the men were there for the purpose of getting off their head and having sex. And anyway, these men, they were sex-pigs, most of them, getting off on extreme sex. There was nothing wrong with that, of course — Eli didn't judge — but at the same time, he wanted the experience with someone sweet, someone his own age (he was still only just over twenty one years old), someone innocent — he wanted someone he could pretend to be in love with.

*

Eli half-dragged half-carried Erik up to his flat by the back stairs. The front stairs may have been easier, but there were windows facing out that way from the other flats. The back stairwell, although someone could have come out their own back door at any moment, did not have windows opening onto it — well it did but they were of mottled glass, and therefore no-one could see. He had also made sure to switch the light over the stairs off before returning to the car to get Erik.

Carrying a man up a flight of stairs wasn't easy. He had at first tried the fireman's lift, but even though Erik was as light as a feather, he was also lanky, and he bent at unexpected angles which meant his limbs kept getting in the way and making him flop skew-if in the wrong direction. In the end, Eli resorted to grabbing Erik front on, as if they were hugging, and manhandling him up the stairs, dragging Erik's legs, heels on the ground, between his own legs.

Thus, bandy-legged, he got Erik to the back door. He pressed Erik's body on the door and held it there with his own weight while he fumbled his key out of his pocket. He unlocked the door and tripped through into the kitchen, then, having a bit of momentum going, straight through into the passageway and down to his bedroom. He kicked the door open, stumbled a few steps into the room and launched Erik's body onto the bed, falling on top of him and knocking his cheek on Erik's sharp jawbone. After a moment he wriggled backwards and pushed himself off Erik up into a standing position. He rubbed his cheek and looked at what now lay on his bed. He smiled. He'd done it. He'd got him.

When Eli had first seen Erik, he knew he was the one. He had been at a pub in Collingwood. It was crowded and there was going to be a band later in the night, so it was filling up even more. Erik had been with a group of friends. He was sweet, he was cute, he had a way of flopping his hair down between him and whoever he was talking to and either looking through it or at something else entirely. He seemed prickly and awkward, unable to make eye contact even with his own friends — so shy, so apologetic, so utterly hopeless. Something about how vulnerable he was electrified Eli — he was just the right type. In fact, he was the one.

Eli had a zip-lock bag of powdered Rohypnol in his pocket that night, and if he got the chance he intended to use it. But it didn't pan out that way. He followed Erik into the band room and stood close behind him. The crowd, when they gathered, had pressed them together. Eli had allowed himself to casually touch against Erik, dancing, moving against him even, but he hadn't pushed it, hadn't tried anything — this one he wanted to save up. Erik had never turned around, had never noticed him, Eli was sure of that, and that was just the way he wanted it.

He had followed Erik and his friends on to another venue, a gay club, when someone came up to him and jogged him in the arm. It was one of Erik's friends. Eli wasn't sure, but he may have sold him drugs before. He recognised the face.

'Hey,' this guy had said. He was a Spanish looking guy, soft, Eli thought. Not a threat.

'Hey,' Eli nodded at the guy, then turned away and said that he wasn't carrying anything tonight. The man ignored him, perhaps didn't even hear.

'You've been watching us,' he said.

Eli turned back. The guy was smiling.

'Nah,' Eli said.

'I can introduce you to him if you like. None of us have had any luck.'

'Nah,' Eli said again, and then he moved away and, after a moment, put his hands in his pockets and sloped out. The last thing he wanted was to be introduced.

*

Eli went back and closed the back door, locked it, then returned to the bedroom. Apart from Erik's body on the bed, it was like a teenager's room, a complete mess. There were posters, there were clothes over every surface, there were plates and glasses and cups, all dirty, some with food still on them or in them. There was a games console, a TV screen, an electric guitar on a stand, amps, cords, a laptop, hand-weights, and a number of tubes of lube. The bed beneath Erik was unmade and the pillows had a dirty mark on the middle of each of them.

Eli stood at the end of the bed and looked at Erik for a long time. He watched the slight rise and fall of his chest. He noticed a growing flush along Erik's jaw where his own cheekbone had clashed with it. Erik's lips were slightly parted — a little sliver of teeth was visible, and beyond that his tongue, the sweet pink of his insides. Also, more disturbingly, his eyes were slightly open. They were just little slits really, but Eli could see the lower curve of the iris — not the pupil, just the iris. It freaked him out and galvanised him into action. The first thing he must do is close Erik's eyes properly. He put one knee on the mattress beside the body on his bed, leaned forward, and with his pointer and second finger dragged the eyelids down over the eyes.

This close he could smell Erik, a sweaty smell, the smell of unclean hair, overlaid with a lot of kitchen smells. He smelt like a faulty exhaust fan.

The next thing to do was get him naked, so Eli set about slowly undressing Erik's unresponsive body. He unzipped the hoodie, then, rolling Erik from side to side, slipped it off first one arm and then the other and threw it on the floor beside the bed. He sat him up, lifted the Bruce Lee teeshirt up and over his head, then let him slump back on the bed out of the arms of it. He unbuckled Erik's belt, pulled it out of the belt-loops and flung it on the floor. He popped open the buttons on the fly of Erik's jeans, lifted Erik's feet, took off first one shoe and then the other, one sock and then the other, then gripped the ankle of each leg of the jeans and hoiked them down. It took a bit of doing, and he nearly pulled Erik off the bed in the process, but eventually they came down. Lastly, he grabbed the band of Erik's underwear and tugged it down his legs and off over his feet.

There he was, pale and entirely naked, eyes closed, limbs rag-doll random on the bed, his chest rising and falling slightly. He was really quite skinny, Eli thought. There wasn't a bit of muscle on him, apart from those sinewy little arms, with tight little biceps like chicken thigh fillets. Eli could see the bow of his clavicle, his lower ribs, his hip-bones. He could trace every bit of the skeleton beneath the skin. Erik's skin was pale, but pinkish-coloured here and there. He had a thin dusting of hair between his nipples, under his arms, at his crotch and over his legs, but otherwise was hairless. He was circumcised and his dick and balls, at the moment slack and flaccid, were neither big nor small but perfectly average. His nob was bright pink, just like a lolly, a musk stick or, thought Eli, one of those heart-shaped candies with words stamped into them: BE MINE; OH BOY; JUST 4 U. Erik was, to Eli, in this moment, naked, unconscious and unresponsive, utterly beautiful.

Eli was surprised by this. He had not expected to feel this way. He felt — well, yes, he was aroused, and yes he was excited, exhilarated really, that it had all gone off without a hitch, the drugs, the car, the whole thing — but he hadn't expected to feel — what was it? — he hadn't expected to feel such tenderness. Heart shaped candies? What was that all about?

He climbed on the bed and lay alongside the body. Erik's eyes had come open a little bit again, so he had to close them with his fingers a second time. He touched Erik's cheek, then his eyelashes, his hairline, his lips. He touched his neck, the flesh, the bump of his Adam's apple, he felt the sinews. He pressed his fingertips there until he felt a pulse, and when he found it he pressed it, experimentally, to see what would happen, if it would get stronger, pump harder against the pressure of his fingertips. When, after a moment or two, there was no change, he got up on one elbow, threw a leg over Erik's unresponsive body, moved on top of him and kissed him.

Kissing a man who is not able to respond was one of the oddest sensations he had ever experienced, and he loved it. Erik's lips did not tighten, they did not compress, they did not return the pressure — they were merely there, so soft when not puckered up — soft slices of skin and flesh, almost silky. Eli kissed harder and Erik's slack lips slid around over his teeth. He forced Erik's mouth open and his tongue inside, against Erik's tongue, his teeth.

Eli began to feel the intoxication of the moment. His body was responding. His dick was hard. He got up, wriggled out of his clothes, got the lube off the floor and rubbed a good slurp of it over his dick. At first he was going to flip Erik over and fuck him from behind, just like he had with the guy at the chemsex party, but at the last minute he decided to do it face to face. He lifted Erik's legs up, manoeuvred his shoulders under Erik's knees, then fingered lube into Erik's arsehole and slipped his dick in. And as he humped Erik's body he kissed him, feeling Erik's slack lips slide around over his teeth.

Eli came in about five minutes. He collapsed on top of Erik's body and huffed into his neck for a while. When his breathing had calmed, he kissed Erik's neck, then his cheek, then his ear.

He started whispering to him. Endearments at first — silly, pink-candy endearments.

Then he recited a few lines of a song — whisper-sang to him.

He whisper-sang the opening line to the song *All Time High*, originally recorded by Rita Coolidge as the theme song of the James Bond film *Octopussy*.

'All I wanted — was a sweet distraction — for an hour or two,' he whispered.

He had been learning this song on the guitar, doing his own version, changing it from easy listening to something a bit more grim, giving it an edge. He had decided to recite the lyrics rather than sing them. And to whisper-sing those particular lyrics like this, his lips actually brushing the ear of the man he had just fucked whilst unconscious, struck him as appropriate somehow.

'I never intended to do — the things we've done.'

As Eli whispered those lyrics, one of Erik's arms, the one Eli lay on, which had been out-flung and unresponsive throughout the entire sexual act, moved — his chicken-thigh bicep flexed, and his arm came up. His arm came up and he laid his hand on Eli's shoulder.

At Erik's touch Eli flinched. He jumped up off Erik and stood over him on the bed.

Erik's eyes flickered, but he did not yet open them.

Eli started bouncing on the bed, his still-erect dick, slick with lube and cum, flapping up and down on his abdomen. He jostled Erik's slack body up and down as if they were on a trampoline. It struck him as funny, the way Erik appeared to be dancing with him, all floppy and rag-doll, and he laughed, suddenly full of energy, full of love.

He jumped down off the bed, grabbed the guitar and hooked it up to the amp, then climbed back on the bed and, bouncing again, blasted out the guitar riff he had been learning for the song — he had played it to Erik the other night, had sung him the song, hiss-whispered it, which Erik had said was dead sexy.

And all through the apartment building, their neighbours were waking up and banging on the walls, the floors or the ceilings, screaming for Eli to shut the fuck up. Some even called the cops, because this was not the first time that a guitar riff had blasted out of Eli and Erik's apartment at 2am in the morning.

THE MUMMY

The Bellatrix was the block of council flats in Sydney where my grandpa lived for the majority of his life, and where, eventually, he died. His name was Theo which is also my name. His full name was Theodosii with a double I at the end. He was proud of our Bulgarian heritage, and it was hard to forget this as he had a Bulgarian flag, Bulgarian patterned plates, and Bulgarian teaspoons, all hung on his wall in the sitting room of his one-bedroom flat.

I called him *Dyado*, which is grandpa in Bulgarian. His English was not great, and peppered with words that I didn't understand — presumably words in Bulgarian. Sometimes, I could guess these words by context, but more often than not I couldn't. It seemed amusing to me that he would cope well with a sentence, but then get hung up on a really simple English word, a word I thought that everyone who learned English must know, and revert to saying it in Bulgarian. He would know words like *Housing Commission*, but still say tomato, *domat*, with a really guttural accent.

It was the first week of summer holidays when we went to clean out grandpa's flat in the Bellatrix. He had died a couple of weeks earlier. I was a bit dark about going to Sydney because we were supposed to be going up to Queensland for time on the Gold Coast over summer. I was expecting to meet up with mates who were going up there, not that I'd given mum all the details about this. But the first thing mum does when I get home from boarding school is pack us both into the car and take us to Sydney to grandpa's flat.

I don't have anything against Sydney, as such, it's just that I don't know anyone there. We live out in country NSW. My stepdad's a farmer, and I go to a boarding school in Bathurst. I had just finished year 11 at the time, and had come home for summer off. It'd been a shit of a year, to be honest. I was starting to get completely jack of school and the country and the brothers and the other boarders, and I'd only just scraped through. I'm not particularly academically minded, although I was scraping by in most things — even so, the prospect of slogging through another year at school was depressing me. I wasn't sure at the time but I presumed I'd do engineering at uni, not because I particularly wanted to, but because my mum and stepdad were pretty much adamant that I go to uni and I had to think up something to tell the careers teacher. To be honest, the only reason I agreed to go through with year 12 at all was because I was biding my time to negotiate a year off before uni to backpack around and see if I could find something to do before I had to come back. I also wouldn't mind seeing a bit of the world, you know? I haven't been out of Australia at all, unless you count New Zealand — we went on a ski trip in year 10. But I'd always wanted to see Machu Picchu, the running of the bulls, that sort of stuff. Check out the pyramids. I guess I'd go and have a look at Bulgaria if it's still there. Is it? I'm not much good at geography.

I have a bit of a scattered family. My dad left when I was only a kid. He was quite a bit older than mum and he had kids from a previous marriage, so I have two adult half-brothers and a half-sister, although we don't have much to do with them. Then, after a few tough years, mum got married again, to a farmer in central New South Wales, so I've also got a brother and a sister who are only 3 and 5. I'm in the middle of them all, a little bit from column a and a little bit from column b. I don't really fit anywhere. Dad doesn't appear to want to have much to do with me, if a lifetime of no contact is anything to go by, and mum, while she has never ever said this, and I don't think would even dare admit it, would probably prefer it if it was just my stepdad, her and their two kids.

To be honest, even though he could barely speak English and I couldn't speak Bulgarian, for a while there it felt like I had the most in common with my *Dyado*. After dad left and mum shacked up with my stepdad, I was shipped off to his place pretty regularly. I spent a lot of school holidays in Sydney with him there at the Bellatrix, skateboarding on the steps out the front with some other no-hoper kids, hanging out in the city, or down at the beaches in the summer. We got into a little bit of trouble together, but nothing all that bad — we were pretty innocent really.

After the first time I was shipped off to stay with grandpa for school holidays, I made mum get him a sofa-bed so I could at least have a proper place to sleep. She did it without argument, without comment, bought it and got it delivered straight to him. I love my mum, and she's done her best for me, always stood up for me with my stepdad or with the brothers at school, but I swear, she's so tight with her money I have to argue to get lunch money from her — I wish she'd at least pretended to be shitty about having to fork out for a sofa-bed. You know?

*

Coming back to the Bellatrix that summer was pretty grim, really. Not only was grandpa dead, which cast a cloud over the whole proceeding, but the flats, as if overnight, had fallen into disrepair. It was subtle but it was obvious. Uncollected garbage. Graffiti tags. It had only been a year since I'd stopped coming during the school holidays, but I guess a lot can happen in a year.

It was difficult to know whether mum was at all sad that grandpa had died. I don't know that I've ever seen her cry. I've seen her angry, that's for sure, and I've seen her laugh and laugh at something on the tele — she's got a great laugh, really gutsy and loud, with her mouth right open, slapping her leg, doing the full pantomime, that it makes you laugh at her laughing — but I've never seen her cry that I can remember. Not at weddings, not at funerals — nothing. And she didn't cry over grandpa being dead.

We were in the town car, the little red hatchback that they used for runs into town. It wasn't used to being driven all the way into Sydney and the motor, when mum turned it off was clicking and stinking up a storm. We pulled up in the street in front of the flats and I got out and looked up.

The Bellatrix was the sort of thing they built housing commission flats like back in the 70s — they call it Brutalist, apparently, and I can see why. This one looked like a whole lot of glass fronted cement TV sets stacked one on top of the other. There was a visible lip of concrete on the bottom of each box, and a recessed join at the top, as if each box had been made off-site and lip-and-joint stacked together on site later. I don't know, but perhaps that's precisely how it was done. It's odd to think of cranes lifting these boxes into place one by one, each with a one-bedroom flat inside it, perhaps fully furnished, perhaps with someone already living in there, reclining in an easy chair, sipping on a beer and watching out the window as their house swung into place.

The location was pretty good. It was, when it was still around, on the north shore of Sydney Harbour, right there in Kirribilli, just alongside the Prime Minister's residence. Every single flat, every single one of those glass fronted boxes, had a perfect harbour view — the Opera house to the left, the city in the middle, and the Sydney Harbour Bridge to the right. They were million dollar views enjoyed by pensioners, the long-term unemployed, and people on a disability pension. I kind of liked that.

From the harbour, or across in the city, the boxes stood out like a bar graph along the peak of the land, rough looking, alongside the more modest art deco mid-rise blocks of flats. Most people called it ugly, an eye-sore, but there was something about it I liked. It was so — well, brutal. It was like a monument. Mount Rushmore or something.

At ground level there was a large stepped concrete concourse with flat steel handrails leading up and underneath a great overhanging slab of cement, which gave the impression of hovering over the steps unsupported. On the bottom few steps, if you looked up, you could see the faces of the glass fronted TV boxes reach up above you. If you peered in under the overhanging slab of concrete you could vaguely see an interior foyer area through glass doors, a depressing little cavern with walls and a ceiling of dark lacquered wood, and the most ugly red and orange carpet, in patterns like amoeba, all of it lit with a murky yellowy coloured light. There had been some sort of modern art on the wall when I had last been there — something abstract, with bold black lines and slabs of primary colours — but now there was nothing.

I knew this entrance very well. I'd spent endless hours skating there, perfecting kickflips — well, trying to perfect them. My eye went immediately to the steps, the rails and the planter box where we used to do grinds and slides, all these familiar spots with their scraped edges, and I felt my first pang of sadness. No more school holidays at the Bellatrix, no more skating, no more kickflips — no more *Dyado*.

*

I helped mum get the flat-pack cardboard boxes out of the back and we went upstairs to grandpa's flat. The minute we cracked the door open it smelt like him, a combination of the spices he used to cook and the bargain-basement cheap-shit cologne he used to douse himself in — but only just a hint. Nothing had been cooked for a while, no cheap-shit cologne had been sprayed. It was like a muscle-memory that smell. He was gone.

Mum and I walked around, taking turns to look in each room, from the lounge room into the kitchen, the bedroom, the bathroom, and finally the weird little elbow of the sunroom. And the view — we checked out that amazing view, sparkling bright, across the water to the Opera House and the Sydney Harbour Bridge. It was as if we had to check that he wasn't really there. And he wasn't, of course. All his stuff was there, left precisely where it was when he had died — dishes in the drying rack on the sink, clothes in the hamper in the bathroom. His bed, we noticed, had been stripped down to the mattress. I checked — the sheets were in the hamper. That's where he had died, in bed. I saw mum eagle-eyeing the mattress for any tell-tale marks or stains, but there were none.

'Right,' she said briskly, rolling her sleeves up — and I mean literally rolling them up. 'Let's do this.'

I exhaled like a horse, flapping my lips. Mum gave me a sharp look for that, so I turned and started putting the cardboard boxes together. We spent most of the afternoon going through things and packing stuff into boxes. Like I said, I didn't see mum getting all that teary or anything, but I did notice her taking quite a few breaks to look through old photos, old letters. I moved behind her one time so as to get a look, and noticed that she was looking at photos of her and dad. While she was distracted, I said I wanted to get outside for a bit of air and a break, and so escaped with my skateboard.

I was planning to do a few kickflips on the stairs, and maybe risk my elbows and knees for a go at a tailslide down the planter box, just for old time's sake, but my plans were foiled right up front. There were a whole lot of people on the steps, protesting. They were chanting and there were signs — most said simply: SAVE OUR BELLATRIX. There was a news camera down on the street, getting shots of the protestors, and presumably this was why they were so raucous and vocal. Someone started up the age-old call and response: 'What do we want?' but as no-one appeared to have rehearsed a response to this, the answers to that were all over the place, and they reverted to: 'Save our Bellatrix,' which became the chant of the day. With fists. The whole lot.

I scanned the faces of the crowd. Some I recognised, vaguely, as being residents of the Bellatrix, but a lot I didn't recognise. A lot of them seemed like ring-ins, with groovy glasses and satchel bags slung across their bodies, hipster types. But they all chanted and fist-pumped equally. Then I saw a face I definitely recognised — a kid we used to hang out with, Jesse. His name wasn't actually Jesse, it was something else, something I can't remember, but as his surname was James, we'd nicknamed him Jesse in a lazy moment, and it had stuck. It was funny because he was the furthest thing imaginable from a Midwestern gunslinger. He was the dweebiest kid, skinny and quiet, the sort to just fade away if anything dodgy was in the wind. He was also a bit pretty and a bit girly, careful of his own skin, you know, so calling him Jesse had an edge to it, and in fact a few of the boys called him Jessica every now and then. We never out-and-out teased him any more than that, and there wasn't anything wrong about him really, but we were a bit dismissive of him, I guess. He was a good skater, though. That I do remember.

When the cameras stopped filming, and the cameramen started packing the cameras back in the van, the whole protest seemed to lose focus — it was obviously just for the news. I walked up to Jesse and stood right in front of him. He didn't recognise me at first, and when he did you could hardly tell the difference. He seemed completely preoccupied.

'Oh hey,' he said.

He was holding a sign at his side, and I'd noticed he'd been right up the front, chanting as loud as anybody else. To be honest, knowing what I knew of him, he didn't seem the type.

'What's going on here?' I asked.

He looked at me as if I was a complete loser.

'I didn't know they were knocking down the Bellatrix,' I said, to make it clear that yes, I did in fact know what a protest was.

'Yeah. They're doing just that. Well, they're going to try.'

He looked like he was considering walking straight past me, as if he was done talking.

'So you're still living here then?'

He looked at me a bit side-eye, and stopped.

'Yeah, I'm still here. We're still here. Nowhere else to go.'

'How's your pop?' We had that in common, Jesse and me, we both lived with our grandpas in the Bellatrix. Me on holidays, him full time.

'Oh he's all right. You know, same old same old. Old fucker.'

'Good to hear.'

He made to walk past me again, then he stopped and turned back with an odd expression on his face.

'Shit,' he said. 'I'm so sorry. I forgot! Your grandpa just died, didn't he?'

'Yeah.'

'Oh man, I'm so sorry. I'm really sorry. I'm just so preoccupied at the moment. I don't — I'm sorry. Is your mum okay?' It was so like Jesse to ask after my mum. He was so soft.

'She's fine. I'm fine. Don't worry about it.' I clapped him on the shoulder. 'What are you doing now?'

'Now?' He looked momentarily preoccupied again, like someone with more on his mind than a 16-year-old should have, but then, as if coming to some miraculous realisation, his face cleared and he smiled. 'Nothing actually. I'm doing nothing.'

'Do you still have your board?'

'Sure.'

So we went for a skate and got some hot chips and ate them by the water down near Luna Park. It was good to catch up with him again.

Jesse had been an odd little kid. I never quite knew what his story was, precisely. You don't tell each other much when you're just a group of kids sort of raggedly hanging out together. We didn't even think of ourselves as friends, really, just spent time together because of a shared location. I think a few of us were school holiday blow-ins, like me. I didn't even know a couple of kids' names.

What I knew about Jesse I knew only through my own observations. His clothes were worn and dirty, and I remember one summer, around the time we all started shooting up in our mid-teens, his denims had become ankle freezers and a little too tight up his crotch. His teeshirts, his hoodies were the same year in and year out. His hair grew down into his eyes and then just kept growing — he wore a backwards cap to keep it off his face. At a glance he looked just like the rest of us — I mean, we all had faded tees and ripped jeans — but if you looked a little closer it was obvious there was no-one caring much for him. He never mentioned a family home, or parents, or even, in the last few years, school — just his grandpa. So I presume that it was just him and his grandpa living together, there in the Bellatrix.

It had been a year since I'd seen him last, but as I said before a lot can happen in a year. Something had happened to Jesse. He'd kept growing for a start. He was head and shoulders above me now. His legs and arms were long and skinny, like skeleton arms. His face had become bonier around the jaw and the eyes, somehow. His eyebrows had got really bushy and his hair had grown out completely and was now long down over his back and shoulders. He wore a red and white bandana, did his shirt up to his throat right to the last button and had the arms rolled right up over his elbows. He still seemed essentially uncared for, but at the same time he was much more put-together than me — a bit of a hippy, sure, but intentionally so. It made me realise that I hadn't exactly done much evolving myself. I felt, to be honest, like a kid standing next to someone who had somehow lapped me and become an adult.

Also, he'd got so damn serious. Man, he was serious. He talked and talked about the Housing Commission and how heartless they were forcing all of the residents out of the Bellatrix.

'You know, they've started having this house lotto thing.'

'House lotto?'

'It's so degrading.' He looked at his feet and shook his head woefully.

'What is it?'

'Residents have to bid on what other council flats they want to move into. They put their bid in a sealed box, and then the Housing Commission Nazis take it away and choose someone at random out of the box, and then, there you go, another one gone.'

'That doesn't sound so bad.'

'Not so bad? Are you kidding? These people have been here all their lives, some of them. My pop, he was one of the first residents back in 1976. Can you believe it? He doesn't know anything else. It's barbaric.'

'Where are you guys gunna move?'

'I'm not going anywhere. There's a resident's action committee and we're pretty sure that if we can get the building heritage listed, we can save it, and no-one will have to move anywhere.'

'What, that concrete eye-sore heritage listed?'

But that was the wrong thing to say, apparently. Jesse started going on about how the Bellatrix was a perfect example of Brutalist architecture, and that it needed to be saved as an example, that it was criminal of the current government to raze great tracts of Sydney's heritage, and that just because a building was no longer considered aesthetically pleasing, it was no reason to get rid of it. By the time he had finished, we'd polished off most of the chips. I chucked the last few to the gulls on the water and stood up.

'I gotta get back,' I said.

Jesse looked at me side-eyed again, as if he expected me to tick him off about getting on his soapbox about the Bellatrix. It was a look I remember him doing a lot as a kid — suspicious and scowling, as if expecting all the time to be mocked or baited. We really had treated him like shit.

*

When I got back mum was sitting in the sunroom with the window open to the view. The sky was getting pinkish behind the Bridge. She had a gin and tonic, her alcoholic beverage of choice, in her hand, and by the look in her eye, as if she was looking at something very far away with great concentration, I guessed it wasn't her first. I'd also noticed on the way through that the kitchen table looked like a bomb had hit it and the cardboard boxes remained mostly empty. She had obviously gone down a rabbit-hole of photos and memories, which, for my mum, seemed unusual.

'Are you okay?' I asked.

She didn't answer for a bit, just looked at the Bridge and the pink sky. It was odd to see my mum like this, thoughtful, pensive, quiet. She was always doing something, organising someone.

'Mum?'

'Where have you been?' she asked eventually, without looking away from the view.

'Out.'

She just nodded, which threw me. That sort of evasion rarely went unchallenged.

'Just catching up with someone I know from when I used to stay here with *Dyado*.'

'Really? A girl?' The usual slightly hopeful inflection.

'No. A guy.'

'What's he like?'

'A bit of a hippy, and super-serious, but okay.'

She didn't say anything else. She had a few snacks on the coffee table in front of her, and rather than do nothing, I had a few crackers.

'Did you and your friend get something to eat?' she asked.

'Yeah,' I said. 'But I'm still hungry.'

We decided to order in, and so I did the deed then went downstairs to the steps to collect it when they rang. We ate in the sunroom watching the sunset, and after tea I got out a few of grandpa's old records, like literally records, and put them on his little turntable. He had some mad stuff from the 70s which mum wanted to listen to — Donna Summer and Sister Sledge. It really seemed to cheer her up, and she sang along to a few songs and even had a bit of a bop when she went to the kitchen to get herself another G&T. It was weird to see her half-cut and letting loose, but I have to say it was so nice that it was just the two of us, that I started enjoying it too.

After a couple more records we both had a bit of a buzz on. Mum didn't know, but every time I was out of the room going to the loo, or changing the record, or getting myself a Coke from the fridge, I put a cheeky little slurp of gin in my glass. It was when I came back from the kitchen one time that things went a bit haywire.

'We might stay here a few days if that's all right with you,' she said to me.

'Sure,' I said. 'I wouldn't mind that, actually.'

'You could spend a bit of time with your friend,' she said. 'And I can get through all this stuff.'

'Sure,' I said again, thinking about my stepdad, and the kids back on the farm, alone. That seemed a bit odd, actually, now that I came to think about it. 'We can't stay for too long, though.'

'Can't we?' mum asked, and there was a bit of a challenge in the words.

'Well, you know they're going to knock these flats down unless they're heritage listed?'

'Oh that.'

'You knew?'

'Yes. Your grandfather sent a letter from the Housing Commission on to me. He'd refused to take two offers of relocation, so they were going to evict him.'

I felt anger rise up inside me.

'Why didn't you tell me?'

She turned away from the view at the sound of my voice. She looked at me, at first in that long-off slightly-pissed way, but then with a sharpness that cowed me. Her lips pressed together, her whole face tightened, and I saw how unhappy she was.

'You? Why didn't I tell you? What would you have done about it?'

She said it like she hated me.

I did the only thing I could really do, I took off out of there. When I hit the steps downstairs my legs felt a bit wobbly from the slurps of gin, but I made it onto the street and down to the jetty. I took off over the harbour on a ferry to Circular Quay, and hung out in town for a while, just wandering around.

The thought of grandpa getting evicted was in the back of my mind all night. Where would he go? Where could he go? To another council flat? It'd kill him. He'd lived in the Bellatrix since they were built in 1976, just like Jesse's pop — long before I was on the scene. I could only imagine how awful it would feel, to be evicted from your only home, at the mercy of a government that wanted to scrap your life and sell the land to a developer.

I mean, I get it, he's dead, so it doesn't matter. But for those few weeks between getting the eviction notice and dying in his sleep, how did he feel? I wonder, too, whether it had anything to do with him dying. Did he decide to die rather than face starting somewhere new at his age? Did he say goodnight to the world, roll over and go to sleep with the intention of never waking up again? Can you do that? It would be amazing if you could, I guess. And like an adult, like my mum, I found myself thinking in my head: 'It's the best thing that could have happened for him.'

As for mum, how could she withhold that letter from me? She knew I was the one out of all the family who was closest to grandpa. She didn't give a shit about him. Dad didn't give a shit about him as far as I knew. It was just me, me and him, the two loners, the two outcasts.

I thought about him a lot that night, wandering around Sydney, then out of the city and down to the Opera House. I sat on the steps for a while — they weren't a million miles away from the steps at the Bellatrix, pebble-dash panels that looked as if they were made off site and lifted into place.

I thought of grandpa sitting at the kitchen table in his singlet, listening to the races, or to talkback, which he loved. He had transistor radios stashed everywhere around the house, one on the kitchen table, one in the sunroom, one on his bedside table, and even one hanging from the toilet roll holder in the bathroom. I remember him drinking beer out of a long-neck bottle while he read the form guide and listened to the races. He'd up-end the bottle and pour it into the side of his mouth, without taking his eyes off the paper, and it'd just glug into his mouth and down his neck, as if it was a drip hanging beside his bed in hospital. Not that he was a boozer, well not all the time. He was, in fact, a simple, quiet, content man. Neat, tidy, house-proud. He'd potter around the flat, cleaning and sweeping and dusting on Thursday every week. I asked him once why he did his cleaning on a Thursday and he said it was because he didn't like Thursdays, and that you may as well do chores on a day that you don't like rather than one you do.

'Why don't you like Thursdays?' I asked.

He shrugged and made an expressive gesture with his hands.

'Because Mondays, you know — everybody hates Mondays. It's not fair.'

I wasn't sure whether he was joking or serious, but I laughed.

He was quite a snappy dresser, and he'd never leave the flat to go to the market or down to the shops without ironing his shirt and squirting a spritz of that awful cheap cologne on. He wore, without fail, one of those cloth caps with the brim at the front — I don't know what they're called. He had about six of them, in different colours and patterns and everything. He was gallant and even slightly flirty with all the female shop assistants, but never in a way that overstepped the boundaries of good taste. He hailed all the men behind the counters, and talked about the weather or the races or how their businesses were doing. I know all this because when I was younger, when I used to come and stay with him, I'd trail along after him, half-bored, half-fascinated. He'd introduce me to all these people behind the counter, people strolling on the streets, people in the lift at the building, everywhere — he would never fail to introduce me.

'This is Theo,' he would say, and everyone would smile and laugh, because our names were the same. One time I wore one of the flat caps myself, and it was like the biggest, funniest joke in the world. It doesn't take much to amuse old people.

And when I left? When I went back to boarding school? What did he do then? Did he drink and listen to the radio and iron his shirt just the same? Who was there to introduce to his friends down at the shops? Who was there to eat a circle of sausage he'd cut off with his knife against his thumb? Did he make his spicy soup with whole vegetables and big gob-stoppers of meat in there when there was just him to eat it? Or were there others in the building, other friends, even a lady-friend, that would come to his neat little flat? I don't know. I hope so, but I don't know. I think not, actually. Somehow, I think not.

How could you evict someone from all that? How could you take someone away from everything that connected them to life? How could they do it to him?

How could I do it to him?

I hadn't come to stay with him during school holidays for the last year or so. Other things had come up. Other plans. Friends. I had a life of my own, and so I had left him to his without a thought.

I lay back on the pebble-mix steps of the Opera House and I looked up at the sky and I let myself feel sad. I may have even teared up a little bit. I might have cried. I'm not ashamed to admit it.

*

On the ferry back later that night, when I judged I'd been out long enough to let mum calm down but not so long that she'd be ropable at me being out too late, I saw Jesse again. He was bent up on an outside seat up the back of the ferry, with his legs up on the seat in front of him. It had been a warm day, but the wind off the harbour was chilly. I went and sat next to him, and elbowed him.

'Hey,' I said.

'Oh hey,' he said. 'Where have you been?'

'Nowhere. You?'

'Same.' There was a pause. 'Hey, I just wanted to apologise for being such a dick today.'

I know teenagers get a lot of slack for not speaking all that coherently, but I seriously believe that, sometimes, 'Whatever,' says it better than anything else. So that's what I said. And that was that — it was done, apology accepted.

I turned away from him and looked off over the water at the Kirribilli shoreline at the familiar stepped shape of the Bellatrix, that higgledy bar graph on the skyline. In one of the windows there were three massive letters, lit up in red lights: SOB.

'Hey — that's new.'

'Save Our Bellatrix,' he said.

'Is that your window?'

'Yep,' he said. Then after a moment, out of the blue: 'That place. It's — it's no good. It's all wrong.'

'I thought you believed in the future — the heritage listing or whatever. Saving the Bellatrix.'

He shook his head.

'Nah,' he said. Then again, 'Nah. There's no future there for me. Not for me. I've gotta get out. Get away.'

'I know what you mean.'

'You too?'

'Yeah,' I said. It was time for me to get away. My dad had his old family, my mum had her new family. I was in the crack in the middle. 'I've just got to get out and start on my own, you know?'

'Yeah,' he said, with some of that zeal I'd seen in him when he was talking about saving the Bellatrix. 'Yeah. Me too.'

'It's time!' I said, imitating his zeal.

The ferry pulled up at Milson's Point under the bridge and we jumped off together and walked up to Bellatrix. Jesse looked as if he wanted to hang around down on the steps for a while, but I wasn't up for that.

'I better go up,' I said. 'Hopefully she's asleep.'

She was — snoring her head off.

*

We stayed at the Bellatrix for another three nights. Mum went through grandpa's stuff and packed everything up. There was nothing left, just a whole lotta cardboard boxes in the lounge-room. It didn't even smell like him anymore. I picked out a few things of grandpa's to keep for myself and put them in my bag — one of the Bulgarian teaspoons, a record we used to listen to a lot together, and one of his radios.

As for Jesse, I saw a fair bit of him over those couple of days. It was different to the old days. Group dynamics are always a lot different to a one-on-one dynamic. There wasn't the same worry about what other kids might think of you, whether you had to toe the line or not, and so we just hung out and it was easy and relaxing. Sure, he was a bit intense, but I just let it all flow over me without listening to it, so it didn't faze me all that much.

It was a hot week so we spent a lot of time at the North Sydney pool, swimming or lying on the concrete steps in the sun. It was here, lying in the sun, that I began to notice something really odd about the way Jesse spoke about his grandpa.

'Can I show you something?' he asked.

'Yeah. What?' I got up on my elbow and shaded my eyes.

He pulled a plane ticket out of his bag and flipped it open.

'I just got it today. I've done it.'

'Cool. Where are you going?'

'Venezuela.'

'Venezuela! No kidding. You're doing it! You're going. Good on you.' I flopped back down on my towel.

'Yeah,' he beamed. 'I'm doing it. Venezuela to start with, then I'll work my way down to Chile, maybe. Somewhere down there. See how we go.'

'Amazing.'

He nodded for a bit, then looked that slew-eyed look at me again.

'You wanna come with me?'

'What?' I sat up and put my hand above my eyes again.

'You said your grandpa left you something?'

'Yeah. His savings. I suppose it'd be enough to get a ticket. And I already have a passport.'

'Do you?'

'Yeah.'

'So you could do it.'

'I could.' I weighed it up in my mind. It was just what I wanted. To nick off out of this country altogether and backpack around some other continent. To get out of here, get my life started away from all my family shit. The prospect, just for the slightest moment, seemed perfect, like your heart's desire right there on a platter in front of you. But that feeling, I reckon it only lasts for a few seconds, as long as it takes your mind to tally up all the reasons not to do it. I wanted to get away, sure, I wanted to travel, to go backpacking, but I didn't want to do it with Jesse.

I looked at his serious face, his intense eyes, his bushy eyebrows, his lank, tangled, long hair. He really thought there was a chance I was going to say yes. It broke my heart.

'What about your pop?' I asked to divert the conversation. 'How will he get on?'

His face fell and he looked away across the pool to the bridge.

'What are you, my mother?'

'I just wondered. I thought you looked after him.'

'I do, all right! I do. Me. No-one else. Just me. I cooked for him, and I cleaned up after him. Me, just me. I shouldn't have had to do all that shit. Not for nothing, you know? It's not fair.' He started shaking his head. 'I've gotta get outta here.'

'Yeah. I get it. I get it.'

'You're not gunna come with me, though, are you?'

I shook my head.

'I can't. I just don't think I can.'

'Course not. I don't know what I was thinking.'

Jesse got up and made his way towards the pool. And it was then, watching him walk away that it occurred to me that every time he spoke about his grandpa he was always mixing up his tense — past-tense, present-tense — his grandpa is, his grandpa was. So was his grandpa up there in that flat or wasn't he? What was going on?

At that moment I got a text from mum asking me where I was and telling me I needed to get back so we could go. I sent her a quick text telling her I'd be fifteen minutes and got up.

I shoved my towel in my backpack and was just about to take off when I saw that Jesse's bag was unzipped. I could see his pants in there, dirty denims, with the pockets gaping. I shoved my hand in and in seconds had fished his keys out and shoved them in my own bag.

I didn't bother saying goodbye to Jesse. There was something I had to do.

*

Jesse's pop's apartment was three levels above mine and a bit further across. I hadn't been there this visit, but I'd been there once or twice back when I was a kid holidaying at the Bellatrix. I knocked on the door. There was no answer. I knocked again. No answer again. I had the key in my hand. I fitted it in the lock, turned it and pushed into the room. There was a smell about the place. That was the first thing I noticed. But perhaps it was just that the whole place was filthy dirty. There were dirty dishes in the sink, cooked-on food on the stovetop, containers of half eaten takeaway on the couch and on the floor, and dirty clothes in little piles on furniture.

The bedroom door was open so I went on through. The bed was empty. The sheets and pillow were rank, unchanged for a long time, it seemed, grey with use. The SOB sign, backwards of course from this angle, took up the entire window. It seemed to have been made out of multiple strings of red lights, like Christmas lights, taped in the shape of the letters directly to the glass of the window. There were about six cords running down to a set of two power strips connected to a double adapter. The whole lot was taped together with black tape and looked as dodgy as all get out, as if it was going to spark and explode at any second.

There were more dirty clothes here, on the floor beside the bed, and shoes kicked off anywhere. I recognised some of the gear as belonging to Jesse. There were a couple of skateboards in the corner. A few other things which I associated with a teenager, but definitely not an elderly man — unless Jesse's grandpa was into xBox.

So where was he?

The only other place he could be if he was in, was the bathroom. The door was closed. I knocked on it.

'Hello,' I said. 'Anyone in there?'

After a moment of silence I turned the handle and cracked the door open. I smelt it immediately. A smell of decay — not fresh but old, very old. And the smell of — was it mice? Mice shit and dust. It was then I realised what I was looking at, what I must have been seeing through the crack — in the bath.

'What the fuck are you doing in here?'

I pulled the bathroom door closed and spun around. Jesse was standing in the doorway. He stepped inside. He stared at me and dropped his backpack by his feet where he stood.

'I didn't kill him,' he said. 'I didn't.'

I nodded my head.

Thinking back, I'm amazed I was so calm. I went all steady and still, but felt twitchy underneath, as if every one of my senses was heightened, like I was seeing and smelling and hearing everything perfectly. It's amazing what a spurt of adrenalin can do for you. And Jesse? What was he feeling? I don't know — how do you know what someone would feel like in that position? The colour had drained out of his face, and his eyes were huge big marsupial eyes, like a lemur or something. And they were imploring me, pleading with me — for what? Understanding? Forgiveness?

He was talking. He stood there, staring at me with those big wet eyes, and talking. He said the same sorts of things he'd been saying to me ever since I'd got there, about how he had to take care of his pop, had been doing so year after year ever since he was a kid, about how he didn't know what he was going to do, how he wanted to stop the Housing Commission from coming into the flat, how he knew he had to get out, get away — I realised he'd been confessing to me, bit by bit, ever since I'd first seen him four days ago on the Bellatrix steps.

His pop had died in his sleep, he told me. He was going to call the police, he said, but then he thought about his pop's pension — it was due in the next day. He'd been managing his pop's money for him for months, almost a year. He had his pop's debit card and his PIN, and he used to go and get his pension out, pay bills, buy food. He also used to give himself a bit of pocket money every fortnight after everything was done. He'd been saving up for a passport. He needed to get out of there, out of the flat, the city, the country, everything.

'I thought — I thought I'd just leave him there, pretend I hadn't gone in and found him. What was another day? I'd just leave him, and the next day I'd go down and get his pension out and get my passport. And then I'd come back up here, and I'd deal with it. But then — but then, I guess, I thought about it and I thought: what's the point of a passport without a ticket?'

He had moved a few steps into the room. Shuffling forward. He'd shut the door behind him, swung it closed without even looking. I noticed that it hadn't closed properly — that it was sitting on the latch.

He hadn't stopped talking.

'So I thought if I could just get a couple more of his pension payments through, I could get a ticket and then take off. I don't — I don't know what I was thinking. So I left him in there. Just left him in there and went on as if nothing had happened. But — but after a few days I came to my senses. I thought: what the fuck am I doing? I can't leave his body in there. So I went in again. I was going to call someone then. But by that time it was too late. He was bruising, his body was bruising, starting to bloat. It — it was too late to call anyone. It was too late. I'd left it too late. I had to put it away. Off the bed. I wrapped him in his sheets and then I put him in the bathtub. And he was starting to smell, so I — I had to cover him with blankets and towels — more and more stuff.'

He shuffled forward. I held my ground, but I felt my muscles tense — every single one of them.

'How long's it been?' I asked.

'Eighteen months. I couldn't do anything — it was too late. And then, then there was the house lotto — they wouldn't let me get a new place for him by proxy, they wanted him to come down into the lobby and bid, but of course he couldn't. So they sent an eviction notice.'

I felt as if I was perched up on my toes, tense and coiled and ready to make a spring. I wasn't scared, not exactly. Those big lemur eyes, they were pathetic. Jesse was soft. But he was also head and shoulders bigger than me.

'I didn't kill him,' Jesse said again. 'I swear. I wouldn't. I looked after him for years. All the time I've lived with him, since the day my mum dumped me here, I've looked after him. Day in and day out. He didn't even know who I was towards the end.'

He stopped talking then, wound down. His shoulders drooped.

'What are you gunna do?' he asked.

There was a moment of silence between us. And then, coiled as I was, knowing the door was on the latch, I made a split-second decision. I decided that I hadn't cracked open that bathroom door. I hadn't seen anything in the bathtub.

'When's your flight?' I asked him.

He breathed out a long sigh. Then he lumbered towards me. I stiffened a bit, but he came right for me and grabbed me in a hug. There was a slump, an abandonment in the hug that surprised me. Jesse really hugged me, properly, like he needed it. And as he pulled away he dipped and turned his head and there was a little kiss in there. Just a little one, as if it was an accidental brushing of lips. It was my first kiss with another guy. I didn't hate it. I wasn't in the least attracted to him, and his hair stank of sweat and pool water, and of course he was utterly mad, but I didn't hate it.

*

When the Housing Commission eventually got everyone out of the Bellatrix, they found the body of Jesse's pop, mummified in the bath under a great mound of doonas and blankets, towels and tea-towels — and doilies. The press didn't mention the doilies, and there was never any photo released that I could find online, but I remember quite clearly seeing them amid the layers covering the body. In fact, I will never forget that glimpse of doilies, because, okay, while it's horrific and appalling to move the body of your dead grandpa into the bath and cover him with blankets and towels so you can continue to collect his pension, it's also sort of sensible in a way, if you get me. But to add doilies to the pile, as if that little lacy extra layer will do anything to stop the smell or to conceal the body or to aid the mummification process — as if it will do anything at all — that's just plain mad.

Jesse? He got to Venezuela, the cops know that, according to the newspapers, but he must have hit the ground running, because they haven't been able to find him as far as I'm aware. The autopsy found that his pop had died of natural causes, so at least I can rest easy knowing I didn't aid and abet a murderer.

I was in Sydney the week before they demolished the Bellatrix. The heritage listing had never come to fruition, everyone had been relocated and the site had been sold to a developer. I went around to have a look. Most of the windows were smashed and boarded up. Graffiti was everywhere. The Housing Commission had put up cyclone fencing around the steps. I could see through and into that horrible cavernous foyer, like a big red mouth. There were couches and beanbags and mattresses and kids push-toys, all sorts of rubbish, piled up just beyond the glass doors as if waiting for someone to squirt petrol on it and flick a lit match in.

I had scraped through year 12, got accepted in to an engineering course, and had convinced mum to let me take a year off to travel before starting. Mum, as tight as ever, said I'd have to pay my own way, but I'm not stupid — I put the money *Dyado* left me aside for precisely this purpose. It's not a fortune or anything, but it'll get me where I want to go.